Plank Brothers

Eric L. Taylor

FIVE COUNT
PUBLISHING
LLC

Library of Congress Control Number: Available upon request

Printed and published in the United States by Five Count Publishing, LLC.

www.fivecountpub.com.

ISBN (paperback) 978-1-943706-23-5
ISBN (e-book) 978-1-943706-24-2

Cover Design by: Shelton

To HTT, LRT, and NET – You all bring so much joy to my life.

Chapter 1

Garrison Smith was hitting his stride.

He dribbled the basketball on a fast break in complete control. The point guard keenly saw the full length and width of the basketball hardwood. Through his eyes, the Wilder County High School gymnasium was his universe, and he was the center of it.

He raced down the court at warp speed, yet his mind was quiet and still. He wasted no movement as his body worked on autopilot from muscle memory and instincts honed by hours and hours of practice.

As Garrison crossed half court, time stood still. He couldn't hear the rabid crowd, though he was aware of them urging him on. He saw his head coach, Pat Van Gundy, standing stoically watching the action. He knew he had Coach's trust to make the right decision. Teammates Andrew Wilson and Danny Fisher were sprinting down the court to his left and right, respectively. Brooks

County Patriot defenders scurried like rats on a sinking ship trying to recover from the errant pass Garrison had deftly intercepted.

Garrison angled a bit to the left, his strong hand. Just like the college and pro point guards he modeled his game after, he kept his head up the entire time surveying the landscape. The Patriot worries mounted as they tried to stop the ball and simultaneously play the passing lanes. Wilson and Fisher waited for slight eye contact to tell them to expect a pinpoint chest pass or a soft bouncer at the last possible second.

Lob Johnson, the six-foot-ten senior center for Brooks County, had sprinted back on defense and anchored himself under the basket. Garrison yearned to "lob" a pass over Johnson's towering frame for an assist, pun intended, but that effort could wait until another day.

After crossing over a would-be defender, Garrison reached the free throw line, slightly hesitating and looking towards Fisher. Lob didn't bite. He held his ground as the rim protector for the defense. The lengthy Lob licked his chops for another highlight-reel blocked shot.

Quick as a hiccup, Garrison lowered his head towards the painted area. Instead of dropping off a pass to Fisher, he went right at Lob, who jumped to block the shot or deflect a possible pass. Garrison, high in the air, put his left shoulder right in Johnson's sternum, knocking the wind out of the giant.

As Lob recoiled backwards, Garrison maintained control and shot a rainmaking floater over the out-stretched right hand of the Brooks County defender. The ball hung in the air for what seemed like an eternity. Then it dropped through the net just as the whistle blew for a foul on Lob. Garrison's body hit the floor, but he did not feel any pain. As he hopped to his feet, he smirked. He had just earned a chance for a three-point play the old-fashioned way, as his dad liked to call it.

The Wilder County Pirate fans erupted in joy! Lob scowled as he struggled back up to his feet. He was used to opposing offensive players shrinking in fear of his intimidating presence, but Garrison did just the opposite. He took it right to the big fella.

He sank the free throw and readied himself to play defense. He glanced up at the scoreboard. The three-point play brought them to within five with only seven ticks left in the third quarter.

Garrison allowed himself to believe for just a fleeting moment. Wilder County had never beaten Lob and Brooks County during his high school basketball career. If they could get over the hump in the fourth quarter it would be a great way to start the season.

Unfortunately for Garrison and Wilder County, that was as close as they would get. Lob took over in the fourth, earning a triple-double stat line of 15 points, 16 rebounds, and 10 blocked shots to lead Brooks County to a 65 to 48 victory.

It was only the second game of the season, but Wilder County fell to 0-2. Garrison was a great scorer and distributor, and they had other talented pieces, but they weren't yet playing like a team. The Pirates still had to figure out that part.

Chapter 2

"Guys, I know tonight really stings," said Coach Van Gundy in the locker room after the loss to the Patriots. "Trust me. I hate losing to Brooks County more than just about anybody since I've been coaching against them for so many years. But, we had some positives tonight that we can draw from. Smith, you played with a ruthless aggression for stretches. That's what we're going to need more of moving forward. Kobe, I know it was a struggle out there, but you competed hard against Lob.

"But we also have to work on maintaining our intensity for the full game. And we'll need to all work on offensive rebounding drills on Monday 'cause we got nary a one of those tonight. So be ready to sweat next week."

Garrison and his teammate and best friend, Kobe Applegate, really appreciated the positive feedback from Coach, but both boys were upset over the loss as they trudged towards the showers. The six-foot-five Applegate served as the team's starting center, and he was usually as big and strong as the other team's center. But that was obviously not the case tonight against the freakishly tall and long-armed Lob Johnson. Applegate was whistled for some questionable fouls that led to an early exit from the game, which gave Lob the opportunity to shut the door on any hope of victory. Kobe also took a few sharp elbows to the chest.

The boys got dressed and chatted as they were exiting the locker room. "Man, Garrison, I had to play Lob *and* the officials tonight. That really sucked," Kobe said.

"Yeah, I'm sure it wasn't fun for you out there," replied Garrison. "The officials treat Lob like he's made of glass."

As Garrison and Kobe slipped out of the locker room to see their families and friends, they were tracked down by the Old Southpaw.

"Tough loss tonight, huh, fellas?" He said.

The Old Southpaw was the county paper's sports reporter who had been in the role forever. No one knew where his nickname came from, especially because he was right-handed. He had reported on multiple generations of family athletes that had come through the school system. Heck, he was old when he covered Garrison's dad's playing days. He was a serious-minded fellow, a dedicated and professional journalist, and a great advocate for the

Wilder County Pirates.

"Yeah, we played hard, Brooks County was just better tonight," Garrison finally responded.

"That Lob, he's a tough customer," continued Old Southpaw. "That was a nice drive you had there in the third quarter, taking it right at him."

Garrison smiled. "Yeah, that was a nice one, but we didn't get the win, which is what ultimately matters."

"Lob's also a little arrogant," Old Southpaw said. "Told me he couldn't wait to move to the next level to really test himself."

Garrison was already ticked by the loss, but hearing that really pissed him off. How did Lob feel about getting knocked on his ass on that one play? Kobe looked at him with a smirk. He would never really let anything faze him but knew what Lob said would light a fire in Garrison. Garrison caught himself before he said something to Old Southpaw he would regret and deferred to Kobe to answer.

Kobe was about to respond when someone brushed by him. All three turned to see Mike Williams, their teammate, walk through the gym and out the side doors. Garrison, Kobe, and other teammates had all tepidly and unsuccessfully tried to make friends with the new transfer from the Queens borough of New York City. He rode the bench thus far for the first two games of the season.

"So what's up with Mike? He sick or hurt or

something?" Old Southpaw asked. Both boys, forgetting about Lob for a moment, just shrugged. "I'll tell you what, that kid needs to play. He's a serious talent, from what I've heard. Combo guard, can really shoot it."

"Really?" said Kobe. "He doesn't seem all that interested in ball, at least from the way he practices."

"Well, you know, it's not like he's had it easy, Kobe," Garrison said.

Williams moved to Starks, Tennessee, the Wilder County seat, from New York under sad circumstances. His mother and grandmother both tragically passed away earlier in the year due to the global coronavirus pandemic. Big-city born and bred, he had to adjust to life as a black teenager in a predominantly white southern town.

"Yeah, that is a sad story," Old Southpaw said. "Hopefully he can pull through and help you guys out. Okay, boys, I've got a column to write. I'll see you at the next game." And with that the Old Southpaw waddled out of the gym, without really getting a quote from either of them.

Kobe and Garrison exchanged fist-bumps and promised to text each other later to meet up for a Friday night out, and Kobe then went off to find his parents.

"Tough loss tonight, champ," Garrison heard over his left shoulder. He immediately recognized the voice of his father, Gary Smith. Gary stood with his wife and Garrison's mother, Sally, and Garrison's girlfriend, Meg

Orton. Gary, an imposing six-foot-four figure of chiseled dad-bod, wore an orange and brown Wilder County Pirates basketball t-shirt, blue jeans, and a pair of 1980s basketball high-tops. Though past his prime with a few grey hairs in the mix, he still looked like he could go grab a rebound or two.

"Yes, Sir, it was. I didn't want to start my final season of high school basketball with two losses, but here we are," responded Garrison.

"Well, you really showed that Lob how it's done, Son," Sally said with a half-smile and fire in her eyes.

Garrison sighed. "Yeah, sure, Mom. I just wish it was in a winning effort." He then told them what Lob had told the Old Southpaw. If Garrison was pissed off, Sally took it to another level. She started scanning the gym looking for him to go give him a piece of her mind. It made Garrison and Gary start to chuckle.

His mom, a buxom blonde stick of dynamite, always livened up every room she entered. She had a knack for making Garrison feel better when he was blue. Sally also possessed a competitive streak that many in the town found excessive. She grew up playing sports year round—soccer, volleyball, and softball. She was always the most competitive person on her teams, and that sometimes caused conflicts with her opponents *and* teammates.

That same passion extended into adulthood. Sally

always had good intentions, but there were stories about her getting into heated shouting matches at PTA meetings, and she had been ejected from a number of Garrison's basketball games over the years, even the rec league games with volunteer referees.

Garrison's intensity and, at times, quick temper were definitely inherited from his mother. Gary always had to monitor his wife and elder son to make sure their fuses weren't lit at inopportune times, lest they explode. He served as a governor for their hot engines.

Meg, standing there between Garrison's parents, hadn't taken her eyes off the young point guard all night long, at least when he wasn't in the locker room. She walked over to her boyfriend and gave him a warm hug. Garrison decided he could wallow in self-pity later; Meg had a way of always brightening his outlook on things.

"You played great, Garrison. I'm proud of you. Do you and the crew wanna go to Chow Station for burgers?"

"Sure, but let me hit Kobe and the boys up. I could use some protein, need to pump up these guns if we are gonna win a game this year." Garrison flexed and kissed each of his biceps before laughing at his own cheesy comment.

Meg rolled her eyes, but playfully punched him in the arm.

"Ouch," he said, rubbing the spot Meg hit him. "I

just told you I have to pump 'em up, don't go hurtin' 'em."

"You are too ridiculous, Garrison," Sally said. "You two have fun, and don't be out too late."

Chapter 3

Chow Station was a town institution before and after ball-games of any significance. You were bound to always find an assortment of Wilder County "bigwigs": the mayor, city council members, business professionals, and other such dignitaries.

Rumor has it Tennessee Volunteers legend Peyton Manning was in Starks years ago, and he stopped by Chow Station for a burger. There once was a picture of Peyton from that night eating an onion ring and posing with the locals in a frame on the wall. However, it had been stolen one night during a post-game winning celebration at the burger joint after the Pirates football team advanced in the playoffs.

Following the loss to Brooks County, Garrison Smith, Meg Orton, Kobe Applegate, Kobe's girlfriend Riley Jordan, Andrew Wilson, and Danny Fisher took their seats at Chow Station around a table in the front dining room area. The restaurant buzzed with a palpable energy beyond the melancholy teenagers. Servers ran around feverishly taking orders and delivering ice-cold beverages to tables. The line cooks yelled out orders and whistled from the lively kitchen as plates of burgers, chicken tenders, and nachos clinked together in the expo window.

Meg spotted Mike Williams, one of the only patrons—outside some of the staff—wearing a neck gaiter up over his mouth and nose, sitting in a corner booth at the very back of the restaurant with his aunt and uncle.

Making eye contact with Danny, Meg looked back toward the table where Mike Williams sat. In a low voice, Meg asked, "What was Mike like before his mom and grandmother got sick with coronavirus?"

"He was always pretty quiet when we were kids," responded Danny. Mike's aunt and uncle, Marcia and Joe Taylor, lived in Starks right across the street from Danny's family. He would come visit during summer as a kid and the two would play together. "He loved being outside shootin' hoops and ridin' bikes around town. I could never beat him one-on-one. He could shoot and had a knack for getting to the rim."

Meg scoffed. "I didn't want a scouting report, Danny," she said. Danny shrugged, and offered a dopey smile. "What's he like as a person?"

"What do you want me to say? He doesn't talk,"

Danny said.

"Well, it really is terrible that he lost both his mom and grandmother to covid," chimed in Garrison, to break the tension. "There's no wonder he's always staring off into space or looking sad. Plus, he's had to adjust from life in the big city to small-town southern life. I can't imagine it's been easy."

"He doesn't have any brothers or sisters, and I never met his dad," added Danny. "Once his mom and grandmother passed away, he moved in with his aunt and uncle. My mom told me Joe called Coach Van Gundy to set up a private basketball workout, which is why he joined the team after tryouts. He hasn't said but five words that I can remember, so it's hard to say what he's like now, Meg."

At that point, the server approached the table and took the food order. The basketball players and their girlfriends ordered a medley of fried goodies, because sometimes comfort food is the best medicine for a tough loss.

After the server left to put in their order, Meg looked back at Danny. "Why don't you motion for Mike to come over here and hop in this open seat?"

"Why?" Danny asked.

"So we can get to know him, try to make him feel welcome, like he's part of the community," Meg answered. "Maybe you guys just gotta make an effort."

18

"Sure, I'll motion him over, but he ain't exactly been warm and fuzzy with us," responded Danny as he raised his right hand, made eye contact with Mike and waved for him to come to their table.

Mike tried to ignore Danny, but Joe and Marcia urged him to go over. So reluctantly Mike stood up and trudged towards his teammates.

"Hey Mike, wanna grab a seat with us and help us pound these chicken wings that are about to come out?" Danny asked.

Mike looked back towards his aunt and uncle, then back to Danny. "Um, sure," he replied with the bottom half of his face still covered.

Garrison and his teammates shuffled down the bench to make room for Mike. Garrison was slightly nervous. He and his friends had only interacted with Mike on the practice court during his time living in Starks, so this was new territory. No one said anything for a few moments, so it was getting quite awkward.

Meg, the number one ranked female junior tennis player in the state and a great conversationalist, eventually opened things up. "Mike, I've wanted to ask you about growing up in Queens. Were you close to the USTA Billie Jean King National Tennis Center in Flushing?"

Mike just nodded, so Meg continued. "I actually went for the first time this past summer when I competed in the girls' U.S. Open tournament. I lost in the second round, but it was such a great time! I loved walking around Queens, there was so much to do and see."

Mike finally perked up. "Yeah, I actually grew up in the shadow of old Shea Stadium, and now the Mets' new ballpark. I worked a U.S. Open as part of the vendor team. Arthur Ashe is cool too, but I'm not much of a tennis guy. My mom loved it, so if she could get tickets she would take me every chance she got."

Garrison was amazed, mostly because he had never really heard a complete sentence from Mike. He was about to ask something when Kobe jumped into the conversation. "Hey man, we're all sorry about your mom and grandmother. I can't imagine losing two people so close to me."

Garrison fought the urge to smack his own forehead in disgust. Meg gave Kobe a death stare, to which Kobe remained oblivious. Kobe had a knack for making things awkward. Never intentionally, mind you, he just had the social graces of a bull in a china shop.

"Thanks," responded Mike. He sunk down some on the bench, and the light Garrison had seen in his eyes just a moment before was gone.

Garrison cleared his throat. "Listen, Mike, if—"

Mike quickly cut Garrison off, "It is what it is. Y'all don't have to do this, you know, try to reach out like this."

"We don't feel obligated at all," Meg said. "We want

to chat with you and get to know you, Mike. What about basketball, are you having fun with that? I know the losses suck, but these guys, even Kobe"—she shot him a look, and Kobe smiled—"are great guys, and they gotta be fun to play with out on the court."

"Well, I miss my boys in NYC, no cap. I miss hooping with 'em. I'm sure you guys are great," Mike said, actually looking up to make eye contact for a split second. "But I told Coach I wasn't ready to play in any games yet, so the two losses haven't really meant anything to me."

Before anyone at the table could respond, the assortment of wings, burgers and side items hit the table, and everyone started devouring the food. Garrison kept watching Mike while they ate. He was still upset about being cut off by him, and also, *he didn't care about losing? What's that all about?* Garrison felt his face turn flush as his blood pressure rose like a thermometer in the Sahara Desert. He wanted to grab Mike and shake some sense into him.

Taking a deep breath, he tamped down his fury. Causing a scene at Chow Station was not something he wanted on his resume. All night he kept trying to get a read on Mike, but so far Garrison couldn't make heads or tails of his aloof teammate.

Chapter 4

Garrison rolled over, bleary-eyed from a somewhat restless night, to shut off his phone alarm that blared Drake bars early on Monday morning following the loss to Brooks County the previous Friday evening.

After killing the alarm, he sat up on the side of his bed, stretched his back and arms. As per his normal early a.m. custom, he went straight to Twitter to see if he missed any sports news overnight. He saw something almost immediately; news from the Old Southpaw slapped him in the face.

BREAKING: Brooks County's Lob Johnson has narrowed down his college basketball destination to four: University of Tennessee, Georgetown, Creighton and University of Georgia.

The tweet angered Garrison. The sight of it flared up

his jealousy and sent him into an early morning daydream. He pictured himself staying in-state as a homegrown hero for the Volunteers, hitting big shots at Thompson-Boling Arena and hearing cheers from the rabid Big Orange fans.

He then visualized himself playing at Georgetown for Hall-of-Famer Patrick Ewing. Garrison fancied himself as the next Allen Iverson: An undersized Hoya point guard with incredible scoring ability and elite ball-handling prowess who takes the nation's capital by storm.

Creighton was never on his radar, and Georgia was a non-starter for him due to their SEC rivalry with the Volunteers. Just the thought of donning a Bulldog jersey made him feel traitorous, and he visibly shook off the image in his mind.

Garrison fell back into bed and sank under the covers. He thought about his past interactions with Lob. Two summers ago they were both at a college basketball camp. It was a Thursday afternoon dripping with oppressive Middle Tennessee heat and competitive furor on the hardwood. The players, on day four of camp, were tired of drills and tired of being yelled at by coaches and counselors. Mostly, however, they were weary of each other after hours of intense competition crashing into one another and battling for loose balls.

Thursday finally allowed for some full-court scrimmaging. Lob Johnson locked horns in the late afternoon game on the primary court with Sheldon

Jamison, another top recruit. Sheldon, a senior to-be post player from Graves County, possessed the physical attributes to give Lob trouble. He not only stood six foot nine, he was strong as an ox. Lob, on the other hand, as a baby-faced sophomore, was slightly taller than Sheldon, but was woefully out of shape and probably outweighed him by fifty pounds.

Lob struggled all game. Early in the fourth quarter, he caught the ball on the left block, dribbled into the lane and launched a right-handed baby hook at the basket. Lob normally made the shot nine times out of ten, but this baby hook bricked hard off the left side of the rim as Sheldon Jamison defended on the play. Jamison boxed out and shot up towards the heavens to corral the rebound.

As Jamison ran back down the court, he let Lob and everyone know all about it, "Damn, 'Blob.' I thought you was supposed to be a player. Hey, someone get 'Blob' off this court, he don't belong here."

Garrison watched from the sideline and could see the wave of anger crash over Lob. *Uh-oh*, he thought. He'd seen the look before on him, when they were matching up in middle school when someone joked to his weight.

Lob picked up his game the rest of the fourth quarter, but Jamison's team still won. As the players shook hands, the simmering volcano that was Lob erupted. Jamison had a smirk on his face as the two met. Lob didn't say anything, he just grabbed a startled Jamison by the throat and pushed him across the court and up against a wall. Then in one motion, he scooped up the Graves County center like he was a toddler and body slammed him into a trash can. Lob then delivered one or two quick punches before other players and coaches jumped in.

"That's the last time you call me fat," Lob finally said. And by the look in his eyes, he meant it.

Jamison was helped out of the trash can and to his feet. He only had a minor cut above his left eye, but his ego was deeply bruised.

Lob proved his point even further the next day, the final day of camp. He once again competed against Jamison, but it was a completely different story. He used a wide assortment of powerful post moves mixed with finesse pump fakes and jaw-dropping dunks to embarrass Jamison all day long. To make things worse, Lob stayed in Jamison's ear the whole time.

Garrison couldn't believe it. He'd never heard Lob chirp like that before in all their years competing against one another. He totally shut Jamison down, who was probably the best prospect at the camp. His performance was noticed by numerous scouts in attendance, which shot him to the top of all the regional recruiting rankings.

Fast-forwarding eighteen months to the present, Garrison's blood boiled with competitive fury toward Lob and the Brooks County Patriots. He was determined to beat them in their next matchup. But he did take solace in one thing: He knew Lob must be angry about the big play at the end of the third quarter, the three-point play where Garrison drew contact, hit the floater, and made the free throw.

"I bet ol' Lob is still pissed off about that one," chuckled Garrison as he continued the dialogue with himself. But then he thought about Lob's comment to the Old Southpaw after the game, about how he couldn't wait for better competition.

Garrison's dream was playing college basketball, but at barely five foot eleven and 165 pounds, the big-time offers were not rolling in. A couple of West Tennessee NAIA schools hinted at scholarship offers, and a few mid-majors talked to him about preferred walk-on opportunities. Rick Barnes and Patrick Ewing weren't blowing up Garrison's phone, so his University of Tennessee and Georgetown fantasies were just that, fantasies.

The prevailing thought amongst scouts was that he was too small. He hated that assumption, but then he too thought about his height. His dad was six-four but grew nearly half a foot after high school. Could he be in line for a similar growth spurt? But would that matter to coaches and recruiting coordinators now? He would give anything to be even six feet tall.

Garrison wished in his heart that his athletic future

was as bright as Meg and Lob's. He had to live with the fact that his girlfriend and bitter rival were both better athletes.

Garrison then thought about his teammate, Mike Williams. He couldn't get Mike's words out of his head all weekend. He didn't care about the losses? Garrison couldn't understand a mindset of basketball and competition not being of the utmost importance. While he hadn't shown it yet in practice, Mike had to have some talent. Coach Van Gundy wouldn't have let him join the team after tryouts if that wasn't the case. Combined with Old Southpaw's assessment, why wasn't Mike playing to his full potential? If he were willing to play, he could instantly give the Pirates a spark, an infusion of energy they so desperately needed. This season was Garrison's last high school dance. Mike, a junior, had one more season left. Why couldn't he see that Garrison and his teammates needed him so badly?

On the other hand, however, Garrison had to acknowledge he had no idea how it felt to lose two people so close to him as Mike had experienced. Garrison was extremely close to both of his parents as well as his little brother, Luke, and baby sister, Sophie. Also, he had both sets of grandparents local and fully intact. His support system was incredibly strong, his family financially secure, and his lot in life largely privileged.

Garrison racked his brain for answers swimming in

his head. *How can I help? Is there a Bible verse I could share? A self-help book? Or should I listen to Meg?* She was always pretty spot-on with her advice and had previously told Garrison he had to resist seeing Mike through a basketball lens. Any attempt to deepen a friendship with Mike had to be genuine and organic, not reeking of self-centered motivation. She told Garrison he should simply be there for Mike, listen to him and perhaps even ask for *his* advice. Could he open Garrison's eyes to things he could be doing better out there?

"Whatever," Garrison finally said out loud. If Mike wanted to be there, then he should show it. Meg already had her future laid out before her. Garrison was fighting tooth and nail to establish his, and he needed any help he could get to see that come to fruition.

He finally rolled out of bed and jumped in the shower to ready himself for school. At practice, maybe things would finally change for the better.

Chapter 5

The Pirates' Monday afternoon practice session felt like a pressure cooker as the antsy players filed into the gymnasium to begin their work. With a record of 0-2 overall and 0-1 in district play after the loss to Brooks County, they now prepared to battle another district foe, the Newmarket Bulls. The Bulls had already notched two wins on the season versus zero defeats. If the Pirates were to lose another district game to Newmarket on Tuesday night, an 0-3 start had the possibility of starting a freefall to the bottom of the standings for the rest of the season.

As promised after the Brooks County loss, Coach Van Gundy emphasized rebounding during practice, especially offensive rebounding.

"Most of the defensive players we line up against will whip their heads as soon as a shot goes up. Once they turn their heads so quickly, that gives us an advantage to move away before the defender can react with a box out," Coach Van Gundy said, and demonstrated with his assistant coaches. All eyes were locked in on the coach.

"Guys, we want to find the path of least resistance. Hell, I've watched y'all plenty on tape. You've just stood there when the shot goes up, waitin' on the defender to box you out. You then have to fight over 'em, which tires you out and draws whistles. Use your smarts! Use your quickness!"

Coach Van Gundy, a basketball junkie and standout player himself thirty years earlier at Wilder County, led the players through a grinding, physical practice that included an assortment of rebounding drills: two-on-two box out, reaction rebounding, let it bounce, and others.

Sweat dripped off the players' brows as they bent over to grab their shorts and gasp for deep breaths of air. Their collective mindset focused on getting through the last part of practice: the last-team-standing drill. Essentially a test of mental and physical toughness, the drill consisted of two teams of three players. Coach Van Gundy shot the basketball with the intent of it caroming off the rim. All six players battled for the ball with the goal being an offensive put-back. The team that reached five buckets first was the winner. The losing team had to run wind sprints.

Coach Van Gundy put together a trio of Garrison, Kobe, and Mike in the last round of the day. They matched up against Danny Fisher, Andrew Wilson, and freshman Steph Croom.

Garrison was slightly pissed he and Kobe drew Mike as a teammate in the drill. He had yet to show any intensity through practice, and it was grating at Garrison more and more as the drill went on. The players engaged in a back-and-forth affair seemingly on the verge of a fight every single play. That's exactly what Van Gundy wanted for his winless team—hunger, fight, and desperation. With the score notched at four apiece, the next put-back would be the winner.

Coach Van Gundy shot a brick that bounced high off the rim. The mob of bodies under the basket went up for the ball almost in unison. It bounced to the left and looked to be going out of bounds along the baseline. Garrison yearned to be the hero to win the game, but he frustratingly found himself on the weak side. Mike was within reach of the basketball. Garrison knew if Mike could grab the ball, power dribble and put his rear end into Danny to create space, he would have an easy kiss off the glass to win the game.

Instead, Mike barely extended his arms before seemingly letting the ball bounce out of bounds. He didn't even make a token attempt to grab the ball. That was the final straw.

"What are you doin'!" erupted Garrison. "Is that how they do it in the Big Apple, the big city? Damn soft as Charmin!"

As soon as the words left his mouth, he wanted a

takeback. This was not what Meg had in mind when she had told him to be there for Mike, listen to him and try to establish a friendship. The rest of the team was wide-eyed at the outburst. They all knew Garrison was intense, but he had never really gotten after a teammate like that. He would talk a little trash and try to motivate, but he was not a screamer.

Mike looked like he wanted to be anywhere else in the world. His shoulders were slumped. He was staring at the ground, and looked like he was trying not to cry. Garrison was instantly ashamed of what he'd done. He was about to apologize when Coach Van Gundy intervened.

"Alright! Everyone, I mean *everyone*, on the line for suicides! Let's go," he yelled. There was some groaning, but everyone lined up for the worst conditioning drill ever invented. They had to run from the baseline to the free-throw line and back, and repeat the process to half court, then the other free-throw line, and lastly the far baseline. However, Coach Van Gundy thought that was too soft, so he had added in the top of both three-point lines to the mix as well.

After about a dozen sprints—Garrison had lost count—the starch was out of the situation, and nerves had somewhat calmed. Coach Van Gundy blew his whistle twice, signifying an end to the conditioning. The whole team let out an audible sigh. Danny barely made it to the trash can on the side of the gym where he lost his lunch. Garrison, despite being in great shape, felt like he would have joined him if they had to run even one more step.

Coach Van Gundy called everyone together and preached teamwork and toughness but did not address Garrison's outburst. As the team came together to put their hands in and yell, "Pirates," Coach made eye contact with Garrison and nodded his head in the direction of his office. Garrison just knew he was in trouble for speaking so forcefully to a teammate. After all, there was a different set of rules for Mike.

Chapter 6

Coach Van Gundy walked into his office and plopped down on the leather chair behind his desk. He motioned for Garrison to sit down as well. The sweat still poured off Garrison like he was under an open faucet. It had been a tough practice, an all-out war. The nerves of sitting down with Coach didn't make it any easier for him to calm down and cool off.

Before Coach could utter a word, Garrison started to blurt out apologies. "Coach, I know I shouldn't have gone off on Mike like that at the end. I'm sorry. Showing up a teammate, especially a teammate that has endured what he has off the court, isn't cool."

Coach Van Gundy leaned forward but didn't say anything, so Garrison continued. "I just know how important offensive rebounding is to you and our team. I was just really getting intense and wanted to win the drill. When I saw Mike just watching the ball go out of bounds,

I lost it. I promise I won't ever do it again. Ever!"

That's when Coach Van Gundy spoke up. "Actually, Garrison, I want to see more of that."

Garrison was slightly dumbfounded. *He wanted more?*

"Look at the poster over there," Coach said, then pointed to the side wall in his office closest to the door. Garrison saw a poster of the legendary Boston Celtic, Larry Bird. He'd noticed it before but hadn't paid a whole lot of attention to it.

The poster showed a fully outstretched Larry Bird diving for a loose ball, and on the poster was one of Larry Bird's most iconic quotes: "It makes me sick when I see a guy just stare at a loose ball and watch it go out of bounds."

As Garrison digested the information, Coach Van Gundy continued with his lecture. "How can I have this poster in my office and continually preach rebounding to my team but allow someone to have one foot in and one foot out? Look, you're a leader and a captain on this team, and sometimes you need to hold your teammates accountable. I know they're all your friends and what not, and it's not easy to yell at your friends and demand more."

Garrison was perplexed. "But it's Mike, and I thought we had to treat him differently?"

Coach sighed. "You're right. He's had a rough way to go. But we have to stop treating him with kid gloves, or he's never going to feel like a full member of this team. The only way for him to truly blossom, recover, and develop meaningful relationships with his teammates is to be forged in the fire of competition with us. I've been thinking about this, and your words today served as the sign I was looking for from the Good Lord. If we continue to treat Mike like he's different from everyone else, he'll never heal."

"But Coach, I just blurted that out today in the heat of battle. Meg told me to listen and try to be friends with Mike outside of the game," responded Garrison.

Coach chuckled a bit. "Meg's one of the smartest kids in school, so I'd listen to her if I were you." Garrison himself smiled, and some of his tension was released. "That said, I truly believe we have to take Mike into the deep waters with us, or else he'll never learn how to swim again. This is a cold, cruel, unforgiving world. Just look at the death toll and economic wounds from coronavirus. Mike can't live in a bubble. He has to re-engage.

"Look, I have a ton of respect for Joe and Marcia Taylor. When Joe called me, he told me I needed to take a look at his nephew because the kid could flat out play. And guess what? I'll be darned if he wasn't right. We've probably only gotten fifty-percent effort from Mike. He says he isn't ready to play in a game, but when he is, I know he could help us. And I believe we could help him by nudgin' him out of this comfort zone, this safe space he has created."

So it was true. Mike could *play*. Garrison had definitely suspected it. Hearing Coach say it made it more frustrating that Mike had yet to display his full talent.

"You grew up going to Sunday school, right, Garrison?" Coach asked, changing the course of the discussion. In addition to being the head boys' basketball coach and a teacher, he was a deacon at his church, and often brought his faith into his coaching/teaching methods.

"Yes, Sir," Garrison answered.

"Do you remember the parable of the lost sheep in the gospels of Matthew and Luke?"

"Yes, Sir."

"What happened, Garrison?"

"Well, I believe Jesus said if a shepherd had a hundred sheep and one of them wandered away, what would the shepherd do? Would he allow the one sheep to flounder and only focus on the ninety-nine? Or would he go after the one lost sheep?"

Coach's eyes lit up. "Exactly! The shepherd went after the lost sheep, found it, and carried it back to the rest of the flock on his shoulders, rejoicing! Mike has gone through tragedies that we can't comprehend, but he's essentially a lost sheep. Our team is the flock, and we need to bring him back.

"Mike has clearly been surrounded by resolute,

positive family role models his entire life, from his late mother and grandmother to Joe and Marcia. Don't take the parable completely literal. He doesn't need us or our team to actually *save* him. We just need to help him get to a point where mentally and spiritually he is ready to be a part of this team. If we don't do that for him, we're doing him a disservice."

Garrison's attitude and body language did a one-eighty. He sat with erect posture, nodded enthusiastically, and made strong eye contact with Coach Van Gundy. He couldn't bring himself to be completely honest with Coach, especially after the Larry Bird quote, Meg being in his head, and the biblical passage. But the truth was, he was feeling the pressure.

"I know you're stressed," Coach said, as if reading his mind. "We are a little undermanned, with only you and Kobe as seniors. And I know you want to have a winning season in your last year and get a chance at a scholarship. But have patience, trust in the Lord and your teammates, and all will be fine in the end."

Despite the nice words, he still felt completely stretched out. Even if Garrison played his "A" game every night, they would be lucky to win more than they lost. Plus, he had to see all the accolades and love that flowed to Lob Johnson. But instead of discussing it, he just pushed it down deep in the recesses of his mind.

Garrison thanked his coach for the lesson, then made

for the showers. He spent the rest of the night in deep reflection, mixed in with some homework, talking on the phone with Meg, and time playing with his younger siblings.

He walked in to school Tuesday morning projecting an air of confidence. The whole situation weighed heavily on Garrison, but teachers and classmates had no idea by looking at him. Garrison possessed an explosive temper, but he also had the ability to fence in his demons the way a waffle fences in maple syrup. Like the waffle, though, sometimes he became too saturated and would break apart.

He went to his first class of the day, Geology, and learned about metamorphic rocks. Apparently, deep beneath the earth's surface, temperature and pressure can cause rocks to change. Depending on the rock and the specific pressures and other factors, recrystallization of the minerals could occur, or the rock's original shape could even be vastly altered.

He went to his locker after class with his mind now on geology and rocks and pressure. If ever there was a metaphor for the way Garrison was feeling—or what Mike was going through, for that matter. Right after that thought crossed his mind, he glanced to his right and saw Meg Orton approaching. Meg, who was usually dressed in athletic wear, must've woken up extra early because she wore a long, form-fitting orange dress, heels, dangly earrings and her hair was fixed in a side Dutch braid. For all the young high school students with eyes and a pulse, it was as if the five-foot-seven athletically built brunette with emerald green eyes had just descended right out of heaven.

After picking up his jaw from the floor, Garrison stammered out a sentence. "Meg, hey, you are fine as lemon-lime."

"That doesn't even rhyme," Meg answered. She did not seem amused or happy.

"What's wrong?" Garrison asked.

"Did you yell at Mike at practice yesterday?"

Oh crap, Garrison thought. He neglected to tell her when they spoke on the phone the night before, and now he realized what a mistake it was. "Um . . . yeah, but it wasn't a big deal."

"That's not what I heard. Kobe's in my first period class, and he said you really went at him, and Mike was almost in tears. Did you at least apologize?"

Garrison didn't know how to answer. He had felt good following his meeting with Coach Van Gundy, but realized after Meg asked he had never actually talked with Mike afterwards.

"Well, um, I haven't had a chance to talk with him, and I don't know his cell," he finally answered.

"Do it," she demanded. "How can he feel like you are trying to be his friend if all you do is yell at him?"

Garrison just nodded. He decided not to say anything more, in fear of making things worse for him and Meg. He understood her logic, but it was also slightly contradictory to what Coach Van Gundy had told him the night before.

Meg stared him down for a moment, then she softened a bit. "Now, if I come to the game tonight you better make it worth my while and drop some serious dimes."

"Dimes? You're the only dime I see around here."

Meg rolled her eyes and tried not to laugh at his incredible lameness. The bell rang for second period. As they stood twenty feet apart, Garrison asked, "So I'll see you in the crowd tonight in Newmarket?"

Meg gave him a look as if to say *Of course you will, Captain Obvious.*

Both turned to walk in their respective directions. Garrison had extra steam in his stride. At that moment, he just knew in his heart he was going to crush Newmarket that evening.

The rest of the largely uneventful school day went by quickly. Garrison felt himself falling further and further into a deep, transfixed state while he went through the motions of classes and lunch.

Chapter 7

Garrison sported aviator sunglasses, his best Sunday church suit, AirPods, and a brooding, contemplative demeanor as he stepped on to the team bus for Newmarket. A simmering intensity radiated off him. Danny Fisher was in the middle of telling a riveting story to four teammates as Garrison boarded the bus, but he stopped midsentence.

"Whoa, look out!" he said. "Someone tell the G-man the president's on the other bus; we are just headin' to a basketball game!" all his teammates started to laugh. "Secret Service is in a mood today; we are in for a treat tonight!"

Garrison chose the seat closest to the front exit and sat down quickly. Had he gone any deeper into the bus, he would have broke character and laughed along with everyone else. He didn't want to ruin his concentration or drop his level of intensity. He likened himself to a pit bull at the end of its chain, aching to get off the bus to tear into Newmarket on the hardwood.

Over the summer Gary Smith had introduced Garrison to 1990s West Tennessee rapper Big Daddy Tenn, who rhymed about being, "pumped and extra sharp just like a butcher's knife." Like the old-school rapper, he felt sharp enough to cut through the competition.

Mike boarded the bus thirty seconds after Garrison and exchanged half smiles with a few of his teammates, but he and Garrison did not make eye contact at all. Mike strolled down the aisle and chose a seat nestled in the back of the bus isolated from his teammates. An apology would have to wait until after the game.

Coach Van Gundy always intentionally boarded the bus last. Garrison watched his coach through the aviators. His piercing eyes scanned the seating arrangements seeking out subtle clues about cliques, budding friendships, or potential strife that could turn into team-killing drama.

He peered down at Garrison last. He gave a slight nod, then he proceeded down the aisle, slapping high fives and speaking words of encouragement with his players. He walked the length of the aisle, then strategically plopped down in the rear of the bus right next to Mike.

Mike squirmed in his seat, so Coach began the conversation. "Mike," he said, "this Bulls team we're playing tonight has some talent, but they're largely just a bunch of bullies. Talented players such as yourself can rise above the fray and neutralize their antics. I may put you out there tonight. Our team could use a boost."

"Coach, I'm not sure I'm ready," Mike said.

"Look, if I didn't think you were ready, I wouldn't be taking you down this road," responded Coach Van Gundy. "I know this has been a terribly difficult time for you losing your family and then being forced to transition to small-town life in Starks. Here's what I know, though. You love the game, or you wouldn't be here. And at some point you need to step out of your comfort zone."

Mike didn't immediately answer. Instead he looked towards the front of the bus. Coach Van Gundy followed his gaze.

"Don't worry about Garrison, or what happened yesterday in practice. Use it, if you can, to find some intensity and rediscover your love of the game."

Mike begrudgingly admitted that Coach was right and said he'd be ready to go against the Bulls. He and Coach Van Gundy shook hands.

Back up at the front of the bus, Garrison's mind was on one of his archrivals, John Jolly, the Newmarket point guard. Jolly sported a military style crew cut, mustache, and was built like the old *He-Man and the Masters of the Universe* character, Ram-Man. Basically, he was as wide as he was tall, could bench press a Buick, and was meaner than a honey badger.

Garrison first played against Jolly at a regional church camp the summer before they both entered middle school. It was a casual pick-up game during recreation hours at the camp and mildly competitive overall. That is until Jolly started setting screens with an intensity like it was game seven of the NBA Finals.

The real kicker was Jolly intentionally punched Garrison in the balls as he went for a rebound. The cheap shot led to a near melee—at church camp, of all places. Ever since that moment years ago, the two point guards had been fierce rivals in middle school ball, summer travel ball, and high school ball. Garrison knew he'd have his hands full against Jolly, and he'd have to pay extra attention to protecting the family jewels.

But Jolly wasn't their best player. That was their six-foot-four swing man, Precious Rollins. Plenty of teams have let the name 'Precious' fool them into thinking Rollins wasn't a stone-cold killer on the court. He was a once-in-a-decade talent on the wing. They would need a slew of players to step up in order to have any chance of slowing him down.

Another thing about Newmarket was their gym. It was a very old structure that Coach Van Gundy swore was built before the Civil War. It had terrible sight lines for outside shooting, so the home team had a decisive advantage as they practiced in the gym every day.

The bleachers were incredibly vertical, meaning it felt as if the fans were right on top of the players on the court akin to a gladiator combat scenario. And the fans were ruthless. There were usually tons of mullets in the crowd, and taunts were the norm. They were passionate about their Bulls. Like Wilder County, Newmarket's local government had enforced very few coronavirus-related restrictions, so the Pirates expected a full, non-socially distanced gymnasium.

Finally, the smelly visiting locker room had no hot water, which was a page right out of the legendary Red Auerbach's old Boston Garden playbook. In fact, some liked to call it the Newmarket Boston Garden.

Regardless of all the negatives, Garrison loved playing there. It felt like it had basketball in its bones, similar to a feeling he had when walking into Allen Fieldhouse at the University of Kansas one time when his dad took him there for a game.

Finally, after what seemed like an eternity, the bus pulled up at Newmarket High School. Garrison jumped up out of his seat, turned to his teammates, coaches, and team managers and announced, "We're in hostile territory, guys. Just remember, the great rapper Big Daddy Tenn once said, 'Only the weak need somebody. Shoot, all I need is me and my crew so screw all of you.' It's game time!"

The unexpected pep-talk from Garrison set the bus

into a frenzy, even if they didn't know who the hell Big Daddy Tenn was. Everyone stood up in unison ready to go to war. The bus was rocking side-to-side. The Bulls were in trouble and didn't even know it yet.

Chapter 8

The Pirates entered the gymnasium for their layup line to a loud chorus of boos. The Newmarket Bulls fans were out for blood, even more rabid than normal. But the Pirates were so locked in they didn't even hear the boos; they were unfazed. To a man, the players had a calm sense of purpose. Tonight was going to be the night their season turned around come hell or high water.

Gary, Sally, and Meg were part of a small pocket of a couple dozen Wilder County fans that had made the trip. The locked in Garrison Smith barely noticed them, though. There were no waves or pleasantries exchanged. Anything that could break his concentration was no longer important.

The game started with a bang. Applegate won the opening tip and tapped the ball to Garrison. He crossed half court and threw a no-look laser that hit Andrew Wilson perfectly in his shooter's pocket for a game-opening three pointer. It splashed the bottom of the net.

Jolly brought the ball down the court with Garrison all over him. His defensive fundamentals were perfect: step-slide, step-slide, step-slide, swing! He forced Jolly to dribble into a trap where the usually unflappable Bulls point guard threw the ball up for grabs. Danny Fisher snagged it and quickly got it over to his point guard. The Bulls defense hustled back to take away the fast break opportunity. Coach Van Gundy called a set play, the old slice around the high post. Garrison passed the ball to Applegate at the elbow. Fisher rushed to the top of the key as freshman Steph Croom simultaneously broke directly for the basket. Applegate delivered a perfectly timed bounce pass to Croom who put it in for a layup. Five-nothing Wilder County.

This was not the start the Bulls or their fans expected. Newmarket coach Joseph Elliott called a quick timeout and immediately lit into his team. The home crowd was stunned, lightly murmuring.

Coach Van Gundy took advantage of the timeout. "See! You cut 'em. They're not machines. They're men, just like you! They bleed just like you! They put their pants on one leg at a time just like you!"

Had Garrison not been so locked in he might have chuckled at how much Coach sounded like Duke from *Rocky IV*, Rocky's corner man.

The rest of the first quarter and start of the second

quarter was much of the same. Precious Rollins hit some tough contested shots to keep the Bulls within striking distance, but at the 3:38 mark of the second quarter, the score stood 32-22 in favor of the Pirates.

Coach Van Gundy looked down at the end of the bench. "Williams, go check in, Son." As the combo guard passed by the coach, Van Gundy said, "I believe in you. Go get 'em!"

Williams checked in for Croom. As Garrison watched Mike sprint onto the court, he thought, *What the heck is Coach doing putting Mike in the game!* He knew Coach Van Gundy said they needed to bring Mike into the fold, but he had no idea it would be this soon. Not in a game as important as this one. Garrison looked at his teammates on the floor. The three other Pirates also seemed surprised to see Mike, but it didn't break their focus. Garrison, though, couldn't shake it as he walked over to cover Jolly on the inbounds.

Jolly took the ball, and as play resumed faced up closely to Garrison and softly said, "What's corona doin' out here? Why don't he wear jersey nineteen? You think I could get our crowd to chant: CO-RON-A, CO-RON-A, CO-RON-A?"

"What did you say?" responded Garrison. He couldn't believe his ears.

Jolly's devilish grin showed he knew he had gotten under Garrison's skin with the comment. "You heard me, bitch. I can't believe you guys are puttin' coronavirus in the game. I thought y'all wanted to win."

Jolly was a master at subtlety and mind games, so no one else in the gymnasium had heard their backcourt conversation. Garrison, without thinking, immediately pushed up onto Jolly and ripped the ball out of his hands. Whistles blew and officials rushed in, but before they could get there Garrison uncorked a baseball pass that hit Jolly in his dome from about five feet away. He then tackled the stocky Bulls point guard.

Players and coaches, and even the mascots, rushed the court to form a large scrum. Luckily, Newmarket always had a good number of police officers at sporting events so they were able to keep the vast majority of fans in their seats. Gary physically restrained Sally from going onto the court to fight Jolly herself. She seethed, with veins popping out of her neck. The coaches finally managed to pull the two point guards apart. Jolly feigned innocence as trash started hitting the floor. The Newmarket crowd hissed and booed, seemingly ready to burn the place down. The whole scene was bonkers.

Coach Van Gundy and his assistants eventually dragged Garrison and the rest of the Pirates back to their bench while Coach Elliott regained control of his team.

"What the hell just happened, Smith!" screamed an exasperated Van Gundy. "We're tryin' to win the game, not the fight!"

Garrison was still too angry to answer. His coach didn't push him, just patted him on the shoulder. Order was soon restored to the gym. The officials huddled up, but Garrison knew what was coming. He'd be kicked out of this game and then face a suspension of who knows how long. He couldn't believe he lost his cool, but he also couldn't believe what Jolly said. There are certain things that are off limits in trash talk, and the death of a team-mate's mother and grandmother was certainly one of those things.

The head referee soon pulled together Coach Van Gundy and Coach Elliott. It was a double technical on Smith and Jolly, but only Smith was kicked out of the game. Coach argued his case both should have been tossed, but like always, the refs didn't change their decision.

Coach Van Gundy motioned to his primary assistant coach, Johnny Woods, to take over coaching duties while he escorted his starting point guard back to the locker room. Van Gundy knew all about Jolly's antics, and he also knew his point guard wouldn't just fly off the handle without some semblance of reason.

As the duo made their way to the visitors' locker room, cola cups, popcorn boxes, nachos, and curse words all rained down on them like a monsoon. It was an unbelievable moment. Garrison took the brunt of the damage. Coach grabbed a towel and wiped some cheese off his sleeve. Garrison was covered and wanted to shower to clean off and cool down. He was stopped by his coach.

"So what happened out there, Garrison?" Coach Van Gundy asked again.

This time Garrison knew he had to answer. He sighed, then turned back to his coach. He took a seat on a half-busted locker room bench and recited the story back to his head coach verbatim. Coach Van Gundy couldn't believe it, and in retelling it neither could Garrison. How could anyone, even Jolly, stoop so low?

By the time Garrison and Coach talked through what happened the rest of the Pirates burst through the locker room door. Without Garrison the Bulls had gotten back into the game, cutting the lead to 38-34. But the score was irrelevant to Van Gundy and Smith until they were able to relay the message about what happened out there and why Garrison exploded like he did.

Coach Van Gundy warned the team and Williams specifically that Garrison was about to share an unsettling story. Every person in the locker room sat in stunned silence as he recited what Jolly had said.

"Mike, I completely understand if you don't want to go out there. This type of taunt isn't what you signed up for," said Coach Van Gundy.

Mike was stunned. Just moments before he felt halfway decent for the first time in months. After the death of his mother and grandmother he had forgotten what competitive basketball meant to him. His first-half minutes on the court had triggered something deep within his soul.

Fighting back tears for a moment, he just let it all out and started sobbing uncontrollably. It was as if a dam had opened, and a flood of pent up emotion came rushing out. No one knew what to do. Coach Van Gundy wrapped an arm around Mike in an effort to offer some comfort. After a minute or so he gathered himself and dried his eyes. Then he had a look of intensity none of them had yet to see. And they liked it.

"Garrison, thank you for taking up for me out there. Don't worry about this one, Jolly's ass is mine. Let's go," exclaimed Williams.

The whole locker room erupted! Coach Van Gundy, usually one who delivered lengthy halftime speeches, knew nothing he could say could get them more fired up and ready than they already were.

The Bulls were in trouble once again.

Chapter 9

As Mike Williams walked out of the visitors' locker room and back onto the Newmarket Boston Garden hardwood, only he knew how much he had been holding back. Truthfully, he had been going through the motions in all aspects of life after his mom and grandmother died. His mother, Jessica Wells, and grandmother, Melba Wells, had been his biggest fans from the early days of rec ball at four years old all the way through his sophomore year of high school. In what seemed like a blink of an eye, COVID-19 took that all away from him; Jessica and Melba were gone forever.

He had started to despise the game knowing they weren't going to be there to cheer for him. On the other hand, he couldn't completely give it up. Because even if just for a split second, he found he could avoid thinking about all he lost while out on the court. Then he would hate himself for thinking he could forget about them and fall deeper into the hole.

Unbeknownst to Jolly, he had just dropped a ladder down into that hole, and Mike was finally ready to climb out.

Without taking a single warmup shot or layup, Williams walked out onto the court. He sat on the bench with a quiet intensity and stoically wiped the bottom of his sneakers, a pair of Ewing Athletics Focus x John Starks "The Dunk" in brown and orange with a hint of royal blue. The shoes matched his Wilder County Pirates white uniform trimmed in brown with orange cursive "Wilder County" across the front. Williams wore jersey number three, his mom's favorite number and John Starks' old Knicks jersey number as well.

Precious Rollins inbounded the ball to Jolly, and a stone-faced Williams picked him up immediately. As Jolly crossed the time stripe, he immediately looked for Rollins on the left wing, but Danny Fisher's ball deny defense had the Newmarket superstar all hemmed up. Seeing his teammate swarmed and unable to wiggle free, Jolly decided to test Williams' defense.

Jolly went hard toward the lane with his right hand, crossed over to his left for two dribbles and then spun back the other way into the middle of the lane to launch a right-handed floater. Williams stayed between Jolly and the basket the entire way, perfectly timed his jump and blocked the shot with pent up ferocity.

The ball hit the hardwood with tremendous impact, bounced high into the air and safely landed in the hands of Kobe Applegate. He quickly shuffled the ball to Williams who shot down the court like a rocket. The Newmarket transition defense was in complete disarray, so no defender stopped the ball. Williams took it all the way to the rack. Everyone expected a layup as the six-foot-tall Williams leapt from just inside the dotted line. The young man kept rising and rising and rising until at last he threw down a right-handed slam dunk that stunned everyone in attendance.

The Wilder County contingent exploded in jubilation. Welcome to Starks, Mike Williams!

Gary, Sally, and Meg hugged and pumped their fists. Joe and Marcia Taylor looked at each other with celebratory relief.

Mike ran back down the court, getting high fives and back-slaps from his teammates along the way. He let himself smile. And it wasn't forced, like every other time he'd pretended since the previous spring. It was genuine, and he felt a surge of relief and happiness he forgot existed in the world. He slapped the floor as he and his teammates got set to defend once more, though he knew in his heart there was nothing that was going to get in his way of leading the team to victory.

Garrison was stewing in the locker room, pacing back and forth. He heard the eruption of cheers but had no idea what was happening. As loud as they were, it couldn't be good for the Pirates. It was killing him not to be out there with his teammates. He couldn't take it anymore. He had already showered and put his travel suit back on. Could he sneak in the gym without security or the refs noticing? Garrison was about to try when his dad walked through the door. He gave him an inquisitive look.

"I hope you weren't going to try what I think you were going to try," Gary said.

"What was that noise out there," exclaimed Garrison. He totally ignored his dad's question. "What the heck happened?"

"You won't believe it," responded the elder Smith. He then told him about Mike's block and subsequent dunk to start the half.

Garrison really didn't believe it. "What!"

"Listen, since you've been barred from entering the gymnasium let's hop out to the Suburban and listen to the game on the radio."

"Great idea, Dad," Garrison said. He was glad his dad offered the suggestion. Had he gone back out to the gym, he probably would have only made things worse for his impending punishment.

Father and son rushed out to the parking lot. Garrison tuned the radio to 92.3 WBHG. Dan "The Man" Crews and his color commentator partner, Phil "the Brewmeister" Brulin, were broadcasting the game. They listened intently as Dan and Phil served as their eyes and ears for what could only be described as pure unadulterated basketball carnage. The Pirates outscored them by 30 in the second half to win 92-58.

"Phil, in all my years, I'm not sure I've seen anything like it," Dan said after the final buzzer sounded. "The Pirates laid siege, pillaged, and fired the cannons. All without their captain! Mike Williams elevated his game and his teammates' performances as well. They poured it on the Bulls. Precious Rollins was completely neutralized, and Williams overwhelmed Jolly with his suffocating defense and complete offensive arsenal."

"Right you are, Dan," Phil added. "It was a complete and total thrashing in the second half. Jolly headed straight for the home locker room and skipped the handshake line. He looked utterly humiliated. The Newmarket crowd is in stunned silence, whereas the Pirate faithful are boisterously celebrating and frolicking around the Newmarket gym like it's their own personal play-land."

Garrison rushed back inside to the visitors' locker room where a raucous victory celebration had already broken out. It was pandemonium, an unusually spirited celebration for a regular season win, especially one so early in the season. Any outsider would've thought the Pirates had just captured the state championship, not their first win of the season.

Garrison and Mike came face-to-face in the middle of the locker room. They both looked at each other briefly, then immediately embraced in a tight hug. No words were said between the two, but none needed to be. Players emptied water bottles all over and around the two basketball guards. It was hard to believe earlier that evening the two young men had been enemies. Coach Van Gundy certainly hadn't anticipated tonight's events, but he was one-hundred-percent correct that the crucible of competition produced pressure that brought the lost sheep back to the flock.

The players took brisk showers, but they didn't even feel the cold water. There were zero complaints. The crew then cleaned up the locker room to leave it better than they found it and walked out into the hall. Garrison saw Coach Van Gundy talking with Coach Elliott. Jolly was there too. He was adamantly pleading his case, it looked like. Van Gundy must have told Coach Elliott what Jolly had said to piss Garrison off so much.

Garrison was too excited to worry about it at that point. He and Mike had agreed to take the bus back to Starks instead of riding with their respective families. In fact, the entire team of twelve varsity players, three team managers, two assistant coaches, and the head coach rode back to Wilder County together on the team bus to keep the euphoria and good vibes going.

Coach Van Gundy boarded the bus last, as per his

custom. The team burst into cheers at the sight of their coach. He glanced down to his left as he started walking past the players, relieved to see his two guards sitting together in the front row. They were on the same green vinyl seat finally getting to know each other.

In the first ten minutes of conversation, Garrison and Mike discovered some commonalities. Williams, a New York City native, considered himself an ardent advocate for New York-style pizza of hand-tossed thin crust in wide slices you could fold together and eat on the run if needed. Ironically, Garrison had discovered this style of pizza earlier that school year when he and Meg went to Nashville for a dinner date. They stumbled upon a New York style pizzeria run by a gentleman named Angelo. Nashville had become a hot spot for transplants and out-of-staters over the past ten years, and Angelo was a part of that boom. He moved his family down to Nashville three years ago to open up a pizza shop, and it was a hit from the very first slice.

Beyond the style of pizza, the boys found another common thread, and a rare one at that: Both of them loved anchovies on their pizza. Neither had ever met another person that shared their affinity for the briny, oily, salty, smelly pizza topping delicacy.

"Alright, bro, we're going to Angelo's ASAP," said Williams through a broad grin. "You have no idea how much I've missed New York pizza. The chain joints in

Starks just don't cut it for me."

"Yeah, we'll get a group and go there soon! I can't wait!" responded an almost giddy Garrison.

As the two boys were about to segue their conversation from pizza to another topic, they were interrupted by the unmistakable booming voice of the Pirates' starting center, Kobe Applegate.

"Oooohhh! That dunk was nasty, Mike," yelled Kobe. "It's blowing up on Twitter!"

Five minutes outside of Newmarket, the bus was now in cell phone tower range, back to civilization. At that moment all the young men, who had previously been living in the moment free from technology, plunged their eyes onto their phones and opened their Twitter apps. Sure enough, multiple media feeds, local basketball media types and plenty of others quickly retweeted Mike's blocked shot and dunk sequence that opened the second half.

The Old Southpaw, with 4,562 followers, sent the original tweet with the video attached.

This Mike Williams of Wilder County is a PROBLEM!

For an old man he had a surprisingly steady hand with the camera. At the moment it already had 1,347 likes and 542 retweets.

"Well, that was a coming out party for sure," said Garrison to Mike.

The boys sat in silence for a few minutes, each glued to their phones. After a while, Mike cleared his throat, and made eye contact with Garrison. Garrison looked up and met his eyes, and Mike looked both serious and somber.

"Man, I can't thank you enough for taking up for me out there tonight. You could've ignored Jolly, but instead you punked him out in front of everybody."

Garrison looked down for a moment, not sure what to say. Should he finally apologize for getting after him in practice, or would it feel too forced now? "You remember Zach Randolph?" He eventually said.

"Oh yeah,'" replied Williams. "I wish Z-Bo would've stayed a Knick!"

"He was my favorite post player when he was with the Grizzlies, and my favorite thing he ever said was, 'Where I'm from bullies get bullied,'" Garrison said with great enthusiasm. "That moment really changed my mindset. So, I look out for my guys. No one gets to bully them. Except me."

The two guards laughed and fist bumped. "So, I always got your back, bro, no need to thank me," Garrison said.

By the way Garrison acted, no one could tell he had

been ejected from the game and faced a possible suspension moving forward. The team won, and that's all that mattered to him in the end. When they were climbing off the bus, though, he was dealt a sharp dose of reality. Coach Van Gundy was on his phone, and he could overhear part of the conversation.

"Look, Jimmy, I know it looked bad, and Garrison had no right to attack Jolly like that. But, we both know Jolly's reputation. He has an innate ability to piss off anyone. I swear he could get a monk fighting mad. Garrison swears he was talking trash about Mike Williams' family dying from coronavirus."

Mike read the worry on his new friend's face. "What's wrong?" he asked.

"Coach is talking to Jimmy Nelson, who is part of the governing body for high school sports," Garrison said. "No doubt he's heard what I did by now."

The boys both listened intently. They wished like heck they could hear what was happening on the other end of the phone but were stuck just trying to read their coach's body language. It didn't look encouraging.

Coach was mostly listening, but finally he sighed. "Okay, Jimmy, I understand. I'll talk to him."

"Don't worry, it'll all be good," Mike said. "Once they hear the real story, they can't kick you out for long."

He gave Garrison another fist bump then ran over to Joe's truck. Garrison was left by himself to wonder. He knew of a kid the previous season who was suspended for ten games for dropkicking the ball after a foul call. The ball had hit a cheerleader in the shoulder, and she was fine. He rocketed the ball at Jolly's face then tackled him and almost caused an all-out brawl, which was way worse.

He went home worried his season—and possibly basketball career—might be over before it really ever got started.

Chapter 10

Wilder County High School buzzed Wednesday morning after the Newmarket game. The Pirate contingent had only been a couple dozen fans plus the team and cheerleaders, but akin to legendary events such as Woodstock and the Music City Miracle, everyone, including students and faculty, claimed to have been there for Mike Williams' dunk. This level of school excitement and celebrity status was typically reserved for football and baseball at Wilder County, but on this particular Wednesday, basketball was king. Garrison was slightly jealous of all the attention Mike was getting at first. But word had traveled about the event that jumpstarted Mike's assault on Newmarket, and Garrison was getting some love as well.

Garrison turned the hallway corner after Geology class walking a little taller than normal with all the admiration being showered on the team. As per usual, Meg stood there waiting to greet him. "I waited for you after the game, then you didn't answer your phone," she said.

"Yeah, sorry, you know there's no service out by them hillbillies in Newmarket," Garrison said. "And I got caught up in the emotion of the win, and we all jumped on the bus together, sorry."

"So you and Mike are cool, then?" she asked.

Garrison thought about it for a second. He hadn't actually apologized for yelling at Mike, but it didn't seem to be an issue with him. "Of course! We talked the whole ride home, everything's good, babe, I swear."

Meg still looked a little skeptical, but she nodded and gave him a kiss on the cheek. "Well, hopefully you don't get suspended for chucking that ball at Jolly. I couldn't believe you did it—well, I could, knowing your temper— but you know what I mean. It was kinda hot in retrospect, knowing you did it defending Mike."

"Well that's why I did it, just so you'd be turned on," Garrison said.

That got Meg to laugh, and Garrison did too. However, her mentioning the looming suspension hung on his thoughts the rest of the day. *What if I miss the rest of my senior season? What if college teams stop recruiting me? Have I thrown it all away?* It was a long wait in the pit of Garrison's stomach until he found out his fate. The hands on the clock were stuck in molasses for the remainder of the day until basketball practice.

The last few days had been a wild emotional ride for the Pirates basketball team. Coach Van Gundy clearly recognized that after the Newmarket game. Therefore, on the bus ride home, he had announced that Wednesday's practice would essentially be a glorified shoot-around and film session.

The team filed into the locker room for practice, and Coach Van Gundy immediately ushered them into the adjacent film room. The players settled into their cushy seats as Coach Van Gundy fired up the Newmarket film. The players sat silently with eyes glued to the screen, greatly anticipating the fight between Smith and Jolly so the coaches made sure to take their time breaking down every nuance before they got to that moment. A palpable weight in the air filled the room.

Then suddenly, the moment everyone waited so patiently for popped up on the video screen. You could see Jolly did say something discreetly before Garrison squared up on him, fired the basketball at his head with Dan Marino-esque velocity and then went into a spear that would have made pro wrestler Goldberg proud. Right after that moment, the camera got shaky and all hell broke loose. It was a miracle the police, game officials, and coaches were able to get the train back on the tracks to continue the game at all.

As Garrison sat in the film room and watched it all unfold, he felt a lump in his throat. The footage assured him he had a suspension looming. Yet his teammates were slapping his back and congratulating him. The Pirates knew their senior point guard had their backs. However, if the opposition knew they could get him off his game and fighting mad, would that be used against him moving forward? Garrison cursed his own temper.

Once the film made it to the second half, the Mike Williams show began, and what a show it was! Mike's block on Jolly and subsequent one-handed dunk from just inside the dotted line was highlight-reel worthy every single time. It looked even more impressive on the huge projector screen than it did on a smart phone.

Beyond that play, Mike finished with 20 second-half points, 8 assists, 5 rebounds, 3 steals and 2 blocks. It was a dominant performance. He completely took Jolly out of the game with his killer on-ball defense too. Even though it was a complete beat down, Coach Van Gundy still found some needed improvement areas for every player on the court, Mike Williams included.

As the players concluded the film session and headed onto the court to get up shots, Coach Van Gundy led Garrison into his office.

"Sit down, Garrison," said Coach Van Gundy in a calm tone. "I got an update on your status."

"Yes, Sir." Garrison gulped and grabbed a chair across from his coach's desk. The knots in his stomach tightened even more, if that was possible, and he had a sudden urge to find a bathroom. He studied the floor in front of his chair awaiting Coach Van Gundy to drop the hammer.

"You're suspended the next three games," Coach said. "We have one district game versus Grafton County and two non-district games against Merrimack County and Riverfront High School that you'll miss. Mike will start in your place. I tried to lobby for you to be able to at least be at the games, but Jimmy wouldn't go for that. You'll have to stay home."

Garrison was instantly relieved. At least his fear of missing the entire campaign did not come to fruition. Although it really sucked, he could live with a three-game suspension. He'd be back in time for the holiday tournament, second half of the regular season, and the postseason.

Coach continued. "We both know your actions finally got Mike to wake up. Hell, I wouldn't say this to anyone else, but I'm glad you did it."

Garrison was slightly shocked, and Coach recognized it. "No, I mean it, I'm real proud of you, Garrison. Takes a man to stand up to a bully. Whether you're on the basketball court or you're an adult in a work or social setting, it's always the right decision to confront and stand up against hate speech whether it's motivated by race, gender, or any other such factor. You did that. Not everyone is willing to take that first step, but when they see a peer do it, they're more likely to follow suit. The first person to stand up exudes leadership and the initial action infuses bravery and ideals within the team, group, or organization. I couldn't be prouder, actually.

"That said, once you come back, teams are going to try to test you, get you off your game. You can't let this one incident define you out there. You can't let *anything* unnerve you."

Coach reiterated Garrison's own fears, and he knew he'd have to work hard to check his temper. He couldn't let someone else rattle him like that to the point he let it hurt his team again.

As if reading his mind again, Coach Van Gundy slid some Coach Phil Jackson books towards Garrison. "Read these while you're out. A little 'Zen' might help you calm yourself down." Coach then stood up and slapped Garrison on his shoulder. "Let's go get up some shots. Even if you aren't playing, doesn't mean you can't still get your work in."

Garrison walked out of the office smiling, knowing brighter days were ahead.

Chapter 11

The team bus left late Friday afternoon headed towards Grafton County to play against the Vipers. Garrison was filled with sadness as he watched the team leave without him. He had gone to offer words of encouragement to Mike, Kobe, and the rest the team. It was a toss-up game as both Wilder County and Grafton County were picked near the bottom of the district in the preseason coaches' poll. The Vipers also stood at 1-2 but had yet to win a district game.

As much as it killed him not to be there for his team-mates, staying home to listen and watch the game with Meg and his family wasn't a bad alternative.

Sally Smith prepared a big pan of lasagna, garlic toast, and a fresh garden salad. Sally, once infamous for her kitchen blunders and charred dishes, now made the best lasagna in the mid-state, or at least she did in Garrison's eyes. Meg mysteriously didn't show up until *after* dinner.

Garrison and Meg played with Luke and Sophie, his younger siblings, waiting for game time. Garrison had begged and pleaded all day, and finally one of Meg's friends had agreed to go to the game and livestream it on Periscope for him. He was sure he'd have to do something ridiculous to make up for it, but he could deal with his regrets then.

Meg plugged her laptop into the flat-screen TV, and the live feed showed up in full HD.

Gary Smith laughed "Ah, technology. This is almost better than being at the game. Thank God for you, Meg, otherwise we'd have to just listen on the radio."

Then Dan Crews' unmistakable voice called out to them through the speakers. "I'm also streaming the radio, so you don't have to miss anything," Meg said.

"Well, Son, you certainly are a lucky one, aren't you?" Gary said. "Beauty and brains? Whatever spell you have her under don't let it up. She's way too good for you."

"Jeez, be a little more annoying and creepy, would you?" Garrison said to his dad. He had started turning red in embarrassment.

"It's okay, Garrison," Meg said. "If it wasn't for your mom and dad, I would have dumped you long ago."

That caused everyone to laugh, even Garrison, though it did tick him off just a little.

The game ebbed and flowed, staying close throughout the whole contest. Mike played a solid game at point guard, but he and the team overall had an understandable emotional let-down after getting up so high for the Newmarket game. At halftime, Grafton County led 32-30.

The second half turned into the Kobe Applegate show. The Pirates were cold from outside so Coach Van Gundy rode his post player across the finish line. Williams did a great job of feeding the six-five Applegate, who used deft footwork and an array of nifty dream shakes to drop 25 points on overmatched Grafton County. Wilder County won 70-62 to move to 2-2 overall and 2-1 in district play.

Garrison felt giddy that the team got the win, but he had a slight melancholy twinge as well. The team won a road game without him. *Hopefully Coach Van Gundy and the fellas still feel like they need me*, he thought. Garrison's worry was somewhat silly because Grafton County was a bottom feeder. Wilder County could beat the bottom teams, but if they had any chance of competing for a district championship, they needed all hands on deck.

"I'll drive Meg home," said Garrison at the conclusion of the game. Meg exchanged hugs and good-byes with Gary and Sally.

Garrison and Meg hopped in his truck and headed across Starks to Meg's house. It was only a short drive, so Garrison made sure to go slow to get as much alone time as he could with his girlfriend.

"You know there's nothing I love more than

spending time with your family . . . and you, of course," Meg said.

"Ha-ha, very funny," Garrison said. He took his eyes off the road to stare her down. She didn't bite, and kept looking out the windshield.

"Well, maybe I love kick serves to the backhand side and overhead smashes better, but other than that—watch out! A fox!"

Garrison's head snapped back to the road. He smashed the brakes, but the fox made it to the other side without any trouble. He had reached across to keep Meg from hurling forward out of reflex. He sheepishly removed his hand with a reddening face once he realized where it had landed.

"A fox, huh? Only fox I see is sittin' right next to me," he said, trying to get his breath back under control after the quick shot of adrenaline.

"Oh Lordy, how do you think of this stuff, Garrison Elias Smith?"

The fact she used his full name told Garrison she liked it, as cheesy as he could be sometimes. "I am quick-witted because you pull it out of me. A poet is not a poet without an object of affection. You make me wanna put my jacket down so you can walk over a puddle! You make me—"

"Alright, Casanova," Meg cut him off. "Let's quit while you're ahead. You may want to keep a few in your back pocket for later."

The young couple pulled up in Meg's driveway as R&B softly played through the truck's speakers. Meg slid over next to Garrison and without uttering another word, the two teenagers engaged in a passionate kiss that went on and on and on to the point of fogging up the windows.

Meg finally pulled back. "I've gotta get in the house. What if my dad is watching out the window? I'd hate for your three game suspension to turn into a longer absence due to physical injury."

Garrison laughed. "Your dad loves me! We've watched ball games together, grilled together, even fired shotguns together out in the country."

"Exactly, Garrison. My dad has guns," she said with a grin. "I've gotta get inside."

"Well, let me walk you to the front door at least. Otherwise I wouldn't be the gentleman I profess to be."

Garrison hopped out of his truck, untucked his lumberjack flannel shirt and walked across to the passenger side to open the door for Meg. It was a chilly, mid-fall evening in Tennessee's central basin. Garrison walked his girlfriend to her front door and sneaked in one more quick kiss and hug before Meg entered her home.

As Garrison hopped back into his truck, he switched the tunes from R&B to rap and called his buddy, Kobe Applegate. He answered on the first ring.

"Kobe, you killed it tonight, big man! That was a

clinic!"

"Yeah, Scotty looked over at their coach about midway through the fourth quarter and said, 'I can't guard him, Coach! He's too damn big!' I can't believe he said that, bro," stated Kobe with a laugh.

Scott Poe was Grafton's center, who had gone to middle school with Kobe and Garrison, so they still considered him a friend. For the most part throughout their high school careers, though, he always seemed to have Kobe's number. Kobe had taken it personally and put in some real work in the off-season. It also helped that he grew three inches and was now slightly taller than Poe.

"That just shows how much you've worked in the weight room and on the court, Kobe," responded Garrison.

"Thanks. I did enjoy kicking Poe's ass. Mike was really good tonight too."

"Yeah, with him it's almost like you don't need me."

"Hope you're being sarcastic, G-man," Kobe said. "We definitely need you. When we get y'all together, we're gonna be just fine."

"Yeah, I can't wait," responded Garrison. He never truly believed it himself, but it was nice to hear Kobe, his best friend since they were in pre-school, tell him they needed him out there on the court.

"You're not the only one who can't wait, bud. After the game, Mike told me it wasn't the same without you out there, and we agreed we can't do this without you, bro," assured Kobe.

The high from the two-game winning streak didn't last long, though. Wilder County fell 84-70 to Merrimack and 75-58 to Riverfront the following week. At the conclusion of Garrison's suspension, the Pirates were 2-4 overall and 2-1 in district play with plenty of season left. Mike, Kobe, and the rest of the team played well in both games, but it was clear they were missing something to really compete. They needed Mike and Garrison on the court together, which had only been the case for all of six seconds so far during the season.

This, however, was about to change. Garrison was now eligible, and things were about to heat up on the hardwood in Wilder County.

Chapter 12

Wilder County hosted non-district foe Dalton High School the Tuesday following Garrison's reinstatement. Garrison and Mike greatly anticipated their opportunity to finally step onto the court together for a full game. The excitement extended to the rest of the town as fans packed the gymnasium.

The Dalton High School Racers were not the most fundamentally sound basketball team. They were an extremely athletic bunch that liked to play small ball, press, and get out on the break to wreak havoc on their opponents. Coach Eric Winston served as the Dalton High head coach, and he had been an athletic, fast-breaking point guard during his playing days, so the team's style mirrored their head coach. Before taking the Dalton job he had been an assistant coach at Wilder County. Garrison had never played for him directly but remembered him from some of the summer youth camps. If he didn't play for Coach Van Gundy, Eric Winston would've been a top choice of his to have as a coach.

Coach Winston also had a tremendous way with words as he crafted much of his verbiage from studying wordsmiths such as Walt "Clyde" Frazier and Muhammad Ali. He was a motivator and a favorite of the local sportswriters who knew they could always get an epic quote or quip from him.

Coach Van Gundy knew his team could combat Dalton's style of play by starting three guards and moving Danny Fisher to the bench as sixth man. As his starting lineup stepped out on the floor, it consisted of Garrison Smith at point guard, Mike Williams at shooting guard, Steph Croom at combo guard, Andrew Wilson at forward and Kobe Applegate at center. In the past, Van Gundy had tried to take the air out of the ball and make Dalton play a different style, but tonight, he knew he had the horses to run with Coach Winston.

When the starters were announced and Garrison ran over to shake Coach Winston's hand, the svelte coach had a smirk on his face, as if to say, "So Van Gundy thinks he can run with us, huh?"

Exactly right, Coach, Garrison thought as he returned the smile. *Hope your boys are ready to run.*

Kobe Applegate leapt high into the air to win the opening tip as he batted the ball back to Garrison, who immediately pressed the action. Mike Williams, adept at moving without the ball, darted to the left wing.

Williams feinted toward the lane then feinted back toward the wing before he fully committed to the back-door cut. At that exact instant, Garrison delivered a no-look bounce pass that hit Williams perfectly in-stride and led him straight to the basket for a layup. It was decisive, quick-hitting, and aggressive. Williams pointed at Garrison as a *thank you* gesture, and Garrison gave him a head nod in return. He and Garrison had not played together other than at practice. And there, they never really clicked. However, they found a natural, instinctive chemistry immediately once on the court in game action.

Dalton's three-guard lineup quickly pushed the tempo offensively but were startled to see Smith, Williams, and Croom stay with them stride for stride. Wilder County's guard trio played gambling defense, and Kobe Applegate's presence in the middle served as an eraser if they got beat off the dribble along the perimeter.

The first quarter was played at a frenetic pace at times, and Wilder County, on pace to reach 100 points, led by a score of 25-22 when the buzzer sounded.

After giving his starters a quick breather to open the second quarter, Coach Van Gundy rotated his starting five back in at the five-minute mark. Their first offensive possession was crisp as a freshly starched shirt. Garrison passed the ball to Croom at the wing, and upon completing the pass, he immediately made a UCLA cut to the low post as Kobe Applegate simultaneously flashed to the elbow. Croom reversed the ball to Williams at the top of the key. Williams caught the ball in triple threat, then dribbled toward the wing as Garrison came off a double screen set by Wilson and Applegate. This freed up Garrison for an open corner three that he knew was pure as soon as he released it. Swish!

The Pirates fired on all cylinders, whether on the fast break, secondary break, or in half-court offense. Defensively, they kept up their pressure. As the buzzer sounded for halftime, Wilder County's lead extended to a robust 10 points. The score was 52-42.

The second half was akin to the first half. Both teams played hard, but Wilder County was always one step ahead of the visiting Racers. Their execution a tad sharper, their defense a bit more disruptive. As the final buzzer sounded, Wilder County had eclipsed the elusive 100-point barrier. The final score showed 106-89. The once raucous crowd now exuded a celebratory mood. Wilder County won the game in entertaining fashion.

Coach Van Gundy and Coach Winston embraced in a hug at midcourt after the game.

"Holy cow, Pat! I can't believe you guys were picked near the bottom of your district in the preseason," stated Winston. "Y'all were posting and toasting, slashing and dashing, swishing and dishing! That was impressive. You beat us at our own game of breakneck speed basketball."

Van Gundy could only laugh at his friend and protégé. "Thanks, Eric. You guys have a hell of a team yourselves. You're already playing well, but you'll be peaking by postseason time."

The next morning in the paper, the Old Southpaw, never one to hold back with the over-the-top superlatives himself, was singing the praises of the new Smith/Williams duo. He dubbed them the "Plank Brothers" as they led the plundering of Dalton, forcing the talented Racers to walk the plank.

Smith and Williams combined for 52 points, 15 assists, 12 boards, 6 steals, and 4 blocked shots. The bay area in California may have the larger-than-life Bash Brothers in Mark McGuire and Jose Conseco and the Splash Brothers in Steph Curry and Klay Thompson, but Starks and Wilder County were more than happy with their Plank Brothers.

Garrison was beyond giddy. In fact, he didn't shut up about it. He and Meg had gone out to grab a snack at Chow Station after the game. Meg looked bored the whole time as Garrison recapped the entire game for her from his perspective.

Never had he felt such a pure connection on the court with a teammate. Sure, he and Kobe had been hooping together since they could walk, but this was different. Mike instinctively knew exactly what Garrison was going to do, and vice versa. He couldn't wait to get back out there and see how far they could go together. The possibilities seemed endless.

Chapter 13

The Pirates win over Dalton moved the Pirates to 3-4 on the year and provided a spark for the remainder of the first half of the season. Wilder County's student section burst at the seams and became affectionately known as "the Gallows." The drama club unearthed pirate props from storage which included plastic swords, periscopes and even a wooden plank. They set up the plank along the rear bleachers where they would actually walk it and jump into a large box they filled with packing peanuts throughout the game, especially when opposing teams shot free throws. It was a creative and fully involved setup. Meg Orton also got the girls' tennis team coming to games fully adorned in pirate garb.

One kid even tried to bring a pet parrot in. Security had looked the other way until the bird had unceremoniously left its perch on the student's shoulder and crapped right on the bald dome of an official, who happened to have just made a terrible call against the Pirates. It earned Wilder County a technical, but everyone in the gym agreed it was worth it.

The Pirates closed out the calendar year with a record of 6-1, which moved them to 9-5 on the season at the halfway point. This included a holiday tournament championship in the Central Basin Classic. Smith and Williams went berserk in the championship game, exploding for a combined 63 points and 10 assists.

The team had a brief five-day respite from basketball at the turn of the New Year. Garrison, Mike, and Kobe planned a Saturday night trip to Nashville to eat at Angelo's Pizzeria. Mike and Garrison talked about New York style pizza and Angelo's almost incessantly since that bus ride back from Newmarket, so this trip was a long time coming.

Garrison and Kobe picked up Mike late Saturday afternoon for the drive to Nashville. While on the way to Music City, Mike went into details about his relationship with his Aunt Marcia and Uncle Joe.

"You guys know Aunt Marcia is from Queens, right? She came down to Nashville to run track at Tennessee State—full scholarship. That's where she met my Uncle Joe, who's from here in Starks. He didn't run track like my aunt, but he sure chased after her. She swears he asked her out for two years before she finally said yes," Mike said with a laugh.

Mike went on to talk about his high school and summer league basketball teams in Queens. "Man, check out these two dudes." He scrolled to his camera roll and settled on a picture. "Faruq and Fuad are these two Muslim twin brothers from Zaria, Nigeria. Both of 'em are nearly seven footers with the best damn footwork. Have you guys seen old videos of Hakeem Olajuwon? These guys play like that, post moves for days!"

"Oh, and check out this guy, Bernard Armstrong. That's my dawg. He was so poor he showed up for tryouts with shoes like three sizes too small. His feet bled until coach found out and got him some new shoes. He is probably the best lockdown perimeter defender I ever played with."

Mike was leaning forward over the center console from the back seat now, excited to be sharing with his new friends. Both Kobe and Garrison were leaning in, though Garrison did keep one eye on the road.

"Here's our sixth man back in the city, Jewish kid named Caleb Abelman. You know how coaches always preach fundamentals. This dude is one of the most fundamentally sound guys I ever played with. Could play any guard or wing spot. Did everything great—shoot it, pass it, handles."

Mike kept scrolling, then laughed when he stopped on another picture. "Oh yeah, we also had this floppy-haired white dude who looked like he could be from

Starks."

"Hey now, we rock mullets, no fancy, floppy New York City hair," Kobe said. He tried to keep a straight face, but all three boys laughed.

"Dude's name is Dylan DeBusschere—white name too, huh?" Mike said. "Don't leave this man open from the corner. Threes all day, but he can't guard anybody. We were always willing to trade twos for threes though."

After talking about his old teammates individually, Mike became a little more somber, talking about the civil unrest that gripped the country following revelations of police brutality. "Man, I still keep up with my guys on socials and text, but it's not the same. Coach Jennings, my summer league coach in the city, took all the guys down to a protest. They didn't do any of that riot crap, though. I wanted to be there so bad. Feels like I let those guys down."

Garrison and Kobe muted themselves and listened, allowing Mike to express his thoughts and feelings without interruption. It was obvious Mike missed his former New York City teammates and missed the diversity of living in the Big Apple. However, the conversation also signaled Mike's continuing gravitation towards trusting his new teammates and his new surroundings at deeper levels. Less than a month ago you'd be lucky to get more than three words out of him. Now they could hardly get him to shut up. Not that they wanted to, though. They were loving the new version of Mike Williams.

Once they got to Nashville, Garrison parked his truck in a downtown garage, and they walked a couple of blocks to their final destination. As they opened the front door to Angelo's Pizzeria, a euphoric "Happy Birthday" shout rang out. There was a sea of Wilder County folks there to celebrate with Mike. He froze, unable to process the moment. Tears started to trickle down his cheeks, and he found and embraced Joe and Marcia.

Mike Williams was a proud New Yorker, but he was now also a Wilder County Pirate and one of Starks' own. He made the time to shake hands or hug everyone in attendance, the whole time still struggling to hold in his emotions. But the cathartic exercise finally made him feel like part of the community.

The Wilder County contingent had three chairs waiting on Garrison, Mike, and Kobe with six huge slices, four of which were loaded with anchovies and Canadian bacon for Garrison and Mike. The true New York style quality instantly struck Mike. Angelo was the real deal in his eyes. Mike felt like he was back in Queens, back home. At least for a brief moment.

After a few hours, the party broke up, and the three boys started walking back towards the parking garage.

"Garrison, how did you know it was my birthday?" asked Williams after they made it to Garrison's truck.

"Bro, I have my ways," Garrison said. "If this whole

basketball thing doesn't work out for me in the long run, I might become a private eye."

"Yeah, you're a big-time Dick, Garrison," Kobe said, then laughed.

"I prefer super sleuth," Garrison said. But he laughed along with Kobe.

They made it back to the truck and hopped in.

"We talked to Uncle Joe, who helped set it all up," Kobe said after buckling his seatbelt. "We know how much you miss home. We just wanted to show you how much we cared about you."

"Man, I can't thank you guys enough. This was awesome. You guys didn't have to do this, but I'm so glad you did. Wilder County feels like home, feels like family. My mom and grandma used to take me out for pizza for my birthday so this was extra special," Mike said.

For the first time beyond Joe and Marcia, Mike Williams opened up about his mom and grandmother. He told Garrison and Kobe full details about growing up in Queens, barely knowing his father and his life up until COVID-19.

He spoke about his mom, a nurse, as his hero. She was a hero to many others during the COVID-19 outbreak, on the front lines as she and her colleagues battled the viral scourge upon humanity. She picked up the virus at work and fell extremely ill. She was put on a ventilator and succumbed shortly after that.

Two days later his grandmother, who was already hospitalized, fell victim to the virus. She didn't contract it from her daughter but rather from the local neighborhood market when she was out buying groceries. Jessica's living will listed Joe and Marcia as Mike's godparents who would take custody of Mike if she and Melba were both gone. The two came up and stayed with Mike for a while but returned with him back to their home and work in Starks prior to the start of summer.

Mike then went quiet for a while. Garrison and Kobe got a little emotional. Tonight had been a bonding experience. Mike had finally let go. He got the pain off his chest and shared it with his new close friends. Basketball was secondary. This was real life. He knew his mom and grandma would always be with him, and the pain might eventually begin to fade. It was nice to feel good about life again. Maybe he was turning a corner.

They rode most of the remaining trip home with nothing but the radio playing until they made it back to Starks. Eventually Garrison pulled the truck into Mike's aunt and uncle's home. He gave them each fist bumps, then opened the door. He paused and turned back towards the boys.

"Man, I miss my mom and grandma so bad," Mike said, wiping tears. "I wish they were here. Tonight was so much fun. They would've loved it."

With that, Mike hopped out of Garrison's truck and

made his way into his aunt and uncle's house. Garrison and Kobe looked at one another and exhaled, emotionally drained after pulling off the birthday surprise.

Chapter 14

The second half of the Wilder County season began the Tuesday after Mike's birthday party at Angelo's Pizzeria. Coach Van Gundy delivered a stern message to his team at the resumption of practice. "We need to take things one game at a time, even taking it one possession at a time. Remember, we have lost five games. We're not exactly the 1972 Miami Dolphins."

But he didn't fool anyone. They won their next three games quite easily leading into their second game versus the Newmarket Bulls. The Newmarket game was on a Friday night, so it had extra electricity. Wilder County packed the entire student body in the gymnasium, now known as the "Pirate Ship," and it rocked back-and-forth for tip-off as if it faced choppy seas. The students in the Gallows brimmed to capacity, and other students even beyond the girls' tennis team and drama club dressed in pirate garb and walked the plank. A standing-room only crowd buzzed with anticipation, and several hundred fans the fire marshal didn't allow in due to capacity rules and loosely communicated COVID-19 restrictions gathered outside the gym.

Before Coach Van Gundy gave his pregame speech to the entire team he pulled his two star guards aside, "Guys, we all know we have history with Newmarket and with Jolly in particular. I know he'll try to be an instigator tonight, but you guys have to rise above his antics. Any type of fight or extra-curricular activity will result in suspensions for the rest of the season. I have that on high authority."

Both boys nodded. "You don't have to worry about me, coach," Garrison said. "I've already missed time, and I don't want to do that again."

Mike gave a more thoughtful response. "Coach, I know some people are just mean, and I also know Jolly must have some deep problems himself to act the way he does. I've had him in my thoughts and prayers."

Coach Van Gundy was slightly taken aback by Mike's answer. Kids his age didn't normally show that level of maturity, especially in the cancel-culture mindset permeating society. He beamed with pride for both young men, knowing he no longer needed to worry about any extra-curricular activity out there on the court.

The school superintendent increased the police

presence for this particular game after what transpired earlier in the season at Newmarket. The city and county didn't want to take any chances. As the players walked onto the floor, a quiet calm overtook them. The opposing players exchanged glances, eye contact, and a smattering of fist bumps as they gathered around midcourt. Surprisingly, Jolly didn't make eye contact. He looked squirmy and uncomfortable.

Applegate launched into the stratosphere for the jump ball and batted it back to Mike to open the game. Jolly matched up on Mike, but even novice basketball fans could sense Jolly wanted to be anywhere else in the world.

Mike wasted no time as he crossed over his dribble and feinted left. Jolly immediately bit on the fake, and that's all Mike needed to cross back to his right and nutmeg Jolly in the process. Jolly turned five shades of embarrassed red after the ball went right through his legs. Mike collected the ball on the other side of Jolly and delivered a bullet pass to a cutting Kobe Applegate along the baseline. Applegate, fully behind the defense, responded with a thunderous two-handed dunk. The rout was on from the very first play.

The rest of the game played out as if the two teams didn't belong on the same court. Wilder County led by a comfortable 25-30 points throughout the entire second half, and Coach Van Gundy played his entire team.

Seldom-used guard Faddyss Wood checked in in the fourth quarter and had the game of his life. He hit a three pointer, blocked a layup on a fast break and hit a couple of mid-range jump shots. The Pirates bench and entire gym went crazy with joyous celebration.

Wilder County won the game 82-57. The coaches and teams shook hands without any acrimony, though Jolly still wouldn't make eye contact. The Pirates went into their locker room for Coach Van Gundy's speech. Jubilation abounded.

But before Coach Van Gundy could address the team, there was a loud knock on the locker room door. Andrew Wilson, wearing only a jockstrap and a smile, opened the door to see Newmarket's Coach Elliott and a somber looking John Jolly. He immediately turned to Coach Van Gundy who quickly walked over to the entrance.

"Coach, John here would like to talk to Mike, Garrison . . . really the whole team," said Coach Elliott. "Can we come in?"

Van Gundy was taken aback for a moment before responding. "Sure thing. Come on in."

Everyone focused in on Jolly. All the hooting and hollering ceased.

Jolly's voice cracked as he began. "I know you guys hate me. I play hard and don't make friends out there. My grandma even says I'm a pain in the ass. That's just how

I play." He let out a nervous chuckle. No one else laughed, and it made the silence filling the locker room even more awkward.

Jolly, looking like he may be on the verge of tears, paused to compose himself. "Look, I said some terrible things in our first matchup that caused a fight. I then lied about it. It has eaten away at me ever since. I told Coach Elliott the truth and then asked if I could come over here. I'll make it right with everyone. I just want to say I'm sorry and . . ."

Jolly was stammering and incoherent. Mike wanted to hate him. He had told himself internally, despite what he told Coach before the game, that he would beat the hell out of Jolly if presented with the chance. But now, he almost felt bad for Jolly. He came to truly believe the words he told Coach. So he rushed his rival with a hug, and Garrison joined in.

As the three boys embraced, they all clinched their eyes to hold back tears. The rest of the Pirates team gathered around the trio.

Mike cleared his throat. "John, thank you for coming over here. I accept your apology. No hard feelings."

Garrison composed himself and offered similar forgiveness. At the conclusion, Coach Elliott and Jolly exchanged handshakes and hugs with the entire Pirates team, and they all wished each other well for the remainder of the season.

A weight was lifted off everyone's shoulders, especially Mike's. Love defeated hate. What a night in Wilder County.

Chapter 15

Wilder County's last game of the regular season was at Brooks County against the vaunted Patriots and Lob Johnson. Garrison, Mike, and the rest of the Pirates circled this game on their calendars weeks ago. The Pirates had enjoyed an emotionally charged yet successful season, but they knew they had to compete with Brooks County in order to be considered a serious postseason threat. The Pirates couldn't just beat up on the bottom teams; they wanted to beat the best.

Sometimes in sports, a properly prepared, intensely motivated, and seemingly deserving team can still fall short of its goal. There's beauty to sports, but there are also harsh realities. Sports results don't care about feelings, storylines, or adhering to a socialist script of equal distribution.

The season finale at Brooks County was a reminder of these harsh sports realities. Lob Johnson was locked in from the beginning, and his teammates were on fire from the outside. It proved to be a lethal combination. Everything Coach Van Gundy tried was thwarted. Lob once again dominated Applegate on the block. Garrison and Mike had their worst game together.

On one play in particular, Lob caught the ball in the paint, executed a perfect drop step, and hammered down a dunk on Kobe and a rotating Garrison. As the ball came through the net, it caught Garrison on the left side of his face and left a big red welt that was prominent for the rest of the game. It was a painful visual that represented the outcome of the game. Brooks County was always one step ahead; they won the game 79-61.

Wilder County finished the season 21-6, their lone second half of the season loss being the finale at Brooks County. They had captured the number two seed in the upcoming district tournament, but it didn't make swallowing the loss any easier. However, the silver lining was they were probably on a crash course to play Brooks County in the district tournament championship game. Garrison hoped he would get a third shot at Lob Johnson.

In the post-game handshake line, Lob bent down to whisper in Garrison's ear. "Plank Brothers my ass. Good thing there were a bunch of scouts here to see the real Garrison Smith in action." He then kept it moving on down the line. Garrison didn't even have time to process the words, much less respond.

There were several major college scouts there to watch Lob Johnson, but the second half of the season had given Garrison a boost on the recruiting trail. That evening's performance in Brooks County probably served as a bucket of water dumped on the campfire. *Maybe I'm just not D-1 material,* Garrison thought. Why was he fooling himself? When faced with real competition, he just couldn't get it done. It ate at his insides as he walked back to the locker room. How could they lose again to Lob? Was he really going to go his entire career without beating him? He barely listened to Coach Van Gundy's speech after the game, and seethed the entire time while showering and getting dressed.

By the time Garrison was ready to leave he was in no mood to play nicely with others. He left the locker room and made straight for the parking lot.

Meg caught up to him before he could make it out the exit. "Garrison, I'm sorry about tonight. I know how much you wanted it."

Garrison tersely shot back, "What do you know about how I feel? You're the number one damn tennis player in the state. I'm a tweener, outlier, too short to play major college basketball, close but no cigar. I'm a pretender! You have zero idea how that feels. Why do you have to pretend like you do?"

Meg, shell-shocked at Garrison's words, gathered

herself and fired back. "Here we go again! I can't believe you want to go down this path. You are such a damn baby sometimes! You're a great player who has college opportunities. So what if it isn't going to be at a big-time D1 school?"

"Easy for you to say," Garrison snapped.

"Why, because I have scholarship offers? Big deal, that doesn't matter to me. If you pulled your head out of your ass long enough to see what was going on, and how much I have supported you . . . have you ever been to *one* of my tennis matches? No!"

"Well—"

"Well nothing. You can be such a jerk sometimes, Garrison Elias Smith. I'm done, go feel sorry for yourself without me."

Before Garrison could respond, Meg turned around and ran off. Why had she used his full name like that? She usually only did that with affection. It stung knowing how mad she was. But rather than feeling bad, it only made his mood worse.

Gary Smith had watched his son's implosion across the gym from about thirty feet away. Garrison and Meg weren't exactly in a private location when their verbal tussle went down. He'd also noticed how Lob had said something to Garrison during the handshake line. It had immediately lit Garrison's fuse. Gary knew it could spell trouble, and unfortunately he wasn't able to get to his son before the fuse ran out.

He decided it was time for some fatherly advice. He walked over and put a hand on Garrison's shoulder. "Son, let's grab a late-night milkshake at Chow Station," he said.

It was something Gary had always done with his oldest son. Whenever Garrison would get down or upset about something, the two would ride out to Chow Station for milkshakes. It'd been years since they had done so. After processing what his father said, Garrison's mood further darkened. He wasn't some little kid who needed a stupid milkshake to feel better.

"I don't feel like no milkshake, Dad," Garrison said.

He said it pretty harshly, but Gary didn't budge. "Too bad," he said. "It'll make you feel better. You just got to trust me."

Garrison stood his ground and locked eyes with his dad. Gary again refused to budge, and stared right back at his son. Garrison eventually sighed and relented. He'd already made a scene with Meg. There was no reason to make things worse for himself.

They dropped Sally, Luke, and Sophie at home after a quiet, tense car ride, then Gary pulled the Suburban back out of the driveway. He passed Chow Station, which confused Garrison, but he was still too angry and sad to say anything. Instead, Gary pulled into a convenience store on the outskirts of town.

"Wait here," he told Garrison.

Gary walked back out a minute later with a six pack of beer. *What the hell?* Thought Garrison. He didn't say anything to his dad. Sure, Garrison had snuck a beer from Gary's garage fridge the previous summer, and he'd drunk a few one time with Kobe. That said, Garrison had never been drunk. He wasn't that big a fan of seeing what it did to some of his friends. He didn't like not being in control of what was happening.

Gary drove his son out to their twenty-five acres on the edge of Wilder County. They used it primarily for hunting, but from time to time they went out to camp or hang out and swim in the small creek that flowed through the land. They had a small cabin along the creek. It wasn't much, just a few cots, a fridge, and a bathroom. It was going on midnight when the Smith men pulled up, put on their coats and hats, and hopped out.

Garrison couldn't believe what was happening. He'd lost the most meaningful game of the season, exploded on his girlfriend, and now here he was about to have a beer with his dad for the very first time. They didn't go all the way into the cabin, but instead sat on the picnic table right outside the door.

Gary cracked open two beers and handed one to Garrison. "Son, you had a rough night, huh?"

"Yes, Sir. I—" Garrison stopped himself. He was going to start explaining what happened and make excuses, but realized all that would do was make his anger boil up again. It also seemed by the way his dad was acting, he wasn't looking for any BS from his son.

Gary took a long sip of his beer, then wiped his lips. "Did I ever tell you about my senior year playin' hoops?"

Garrison bit his tongue. His dad at times wouldn't shut up about his playing days. He didn't want to piss off his dad, though. He knew he was in for quite a speech, so he just nodded. "Yeah, I think so."

Gary laughed. "Yeah, I probably have a time or two. Did I ever tell you about your mom's days playing volley-ball?"

"No, I'm not sure I've heard that."

"Well, despite her warm, cheery nature, she can be a bit of a bulldog."

"Duh, Dad." Garrison couldn't help himself, and both men laughed. Garrison took his first sip of the beer. It had a bitter taste to him, but it still felt good going down.

"After we started dating during her junior year I used to go to all her games. For the longest time she despised it because she thought it affected her intensity. Anytime she made a mistake she glared at me like it was my fault." Gary took another drink of his beer, then looked up to the stars. "I never really took notice, I was too busy staring at her ass."

Garrison had been taking another sip of his beer and

proceeded to spit it out all over the grass. "Gross, Dad, that's my mom you're talkin' about," he said.

"I'm kidding, just trying to get a rise out of you," Gary said, and slapped his son on the leg. "I would just offer words of encouragement and cheer her on the entire time. I was quite obnoxious, for sure, but it was all from a good place.

"Later on in the season, during districts, I had something going on and couldn't make it to the game. I can't even tell you what it was today, but it was probably something dumb. But your mom, when she looked for me, and couldn't find me, it totally threw her off her game. They ended up losing the match and didn't make it to the district finals even though they were the top seed."

"So, what are you trying to tell me?" Garrison asked.

"When I saw her the next day at school, she blamed me for the loss and refused to talk to me for a week. Sound familiar?"

Garrison just nodded. He had inherited his mom's intensity, but also some of her temper, so it hit a little too close to home.

"I was mad at her for the rest of the day, until I realized that I had promised her days before I'd be there to cheer her on like I always did. Once I had to do whatever the hell I was doing, I never told her I wouldn't be there.

"I apologized the next day, and the day after that, and

the one after that, and made sure I was there for her. She ignored me for a long time, but I eventually broke her down, and she apologized to me. That was really the last major fight we've ever had, and we've been together for twenty-four years now."

"Okay . . . but what does that mean for me, Dad? It doesn't change the fact that Meg's got it made with her choice of schools. I've got nothing."

"Well, Son, the moral of the story is you need to be there for the people you care about. You and Mike might have had a rocky relationship at the start, but look, what happened when both of you were there for each other? You didn't really have to say anything all touchy-feely, but each of you, subconsciously, knew it would be alright because the other would be there. Same goes for you and Kobe and the rest of your teammates. You guys know that if something happens to one of you, the rest of you got their back.

"That's what Meg's looking for, for you to be there for her. She's there every night screaming her head off supporting you, but you weren't really reciprocating, you know what I mean?"

Garrison thought about it for a while and became slightly ashamed of himself. Why did he let Lob get to him like that? Garrison had talent; those scouts were there watching for a reason. Even though it would be tough, he needed to accept that and let the cards fall as they may.

He then thought about Meg. Had he really been that bad of a boyfriend? Why was he being so petty? He should feel nothing but happiness for her and her scholarship offers. Meg was right. Garrison had yet to watch one of her tennis matches, and he had no real reason for why that was the case. He felt like crying, and he didn't try to hide it.

"Listen, don't beat yourself up about it too bad, G-man," his dad said. "It's not as bad as you think it is. You two are just a couple seventeen-year-olds trying to figure out life. She'll forgive you, but it might take a while. It's easy to see how much she cares for you.

"I love your momma more than anything on this Earth, and y'all are just alike. It's scary, really. I'll be damned if your tempers don't screw it all up sometimes. You have to harness it, Son. There was no need whatsoever to yell at Meg like you did. But now you need to man up to your mistake, swallow your pride, and if you truly care for her, do whatever it takes to make it up to her.

"You may feel down in the dumps now, but look at what you have. We're financially sound, you have a caring girlfriend, a supportive family, and close friends on your team that are basically brothers. You have this town by the balls. Plus, you're going to play college basketball somewhere next season. Worst case, you'll play NAIA ball in West Tennessee. That will be a tremendous experience. Let's cheers to all of that!"

The two men clinked their bottles together. Garrison knew he had a long way to go to fix his personal issues. And making it up to Meg was going to be a whole other ball game. But that first father-son beer, along with his father's heartfelt words, helped soothe Garrison Smith's soul.

Chapter 16

The district tournament started three days after the season-ending loss to Brooks County. The first round was a cakewalk for the Pirates as they doubled up Derry High School 70-35. Garrison and Mike both got back on track, and Kobe Applegate regained some confidence after being decimated by Lob Johnson in the regular season finale. Along those same lines, Brooks County romped in their first game. Lob Johnson didn't even have to play in the second half. Instead, his legs were preserved for later round games.

The district semifinals were a bit tougher for both teams, but again, both pulled through. Brooks County defeated Newmarket, so there would be no third matchup in the district tournament between the Plank Brothers and John Jolly. That set up what everyone wanted to see: A district final featuring Wilder County versus Brooks County at Newmarket's gym. The smart and savvy

Newmarket town mayor had evidently greased some palms to be able to host the district tournament. After all, Newmarket had some great dinner spots, and the town could always use a little extra economic boost from visiting fans during tough times.

The district championship game was slated for a Saturday night. Garrison had to get his mind right that morning. But his fight with Meg was still nagging at him. He had acknowledged he had been acting like an ass. It was eating him up inside. He couldn't truly begin his preparation for the biggest game of his career without first trying to repair his relationship with his girlfriend.

He had profusely tried to apologize to Meg, sent her flowers, and even bought her a new tennis skirt for her upcoming season. Meg had yet to respond and ignored him in the hallways at school whenever he tried to say something. Other kids who witnessed him getting blown off each time in the hallways either laughed at his failures or felt bad for him. But Meg had at least showed up to the first two district games, so that had been encouraging.

Garrison found out the girls tennis team was having a workout Saturday morning, so he made sure he was up in time to go to the courts and watch. He was the only spectator. For a while he felt stupid. *Is this the right thing to do?* He thought. But he was determined to stay and try to speak with Meg's afterwards.

At one point she looked over. She was far away, so

he couldn't see the look on her face. He hoped she was happy to see him, but she never looked over again, which didn't bode well for Garrison.

He watched for a little over an hour before their coach ended the workout. He said "Hello" to all the girls as they left the court, and most said "Hi" back, and wished him luck in the district finals.

Whether on purpose or not, Meg was the last one on the courts. Garrison passed through the gate before she could leave. She stood there looking at him with her arms akimbo, holding her racket in her left hand. Her hair was in a double braid under a Wilder County visor. She looked so incredibly cute Garrison wanted to kick himself for never coming to watch her play before. A thought of what his dad said about staring at his mom's butt popped in his head, and he quickly shook away that gross image. Meg noticed the look on his face, which caused her to adopt a similar expression towards him.

"So . . . this is what a tennis court looks like?" Garrison said.

Meg stared at him for a while without moving or changing her expression. Garrison didn't say anything right away either, but eventually lost the staring contest. He looked down and started kicking imaginary rocks.

"Look Meg, I'm sorry for the way I acted. I . . . um, I mean . . . I was just really pissed after the game, and Lob said some stuff to me that made it worse and I've never beaten him and you were the first person I saw afterwards and I blew up on you for no reason." He was rambling, and knew it, but he kept going. "You're the best thing in my life and make coming to school and stuff worth it, and if I screwed that up, I wouldn't know what to do with myself."

There was a long pause. Meg continued to stare at him. He broke eye contact again. Dejected, his shoulders slumped and he turned to leave. As he did Meg sighed, then finally spoke.

"I just hate how sometimes you blow up like that. I've seen it before, but it had never been directed at me." She had tears in her eyes.

Garrison was happy she finally spoke to him, though even more embarrassed at his own behavior knowing he was capable of making her cry.

"I know, Meg, and I don't think I can ever apologize enough for how I acted."

"My dad told me—after I stopped him from grabbing his shotgun and marching to your house—that I should take some time to figure it all out." She smiled then, and Garrison did too, because if she was willing to make jokes about her dad hunting him down then he knew things might not be as bad as he feared.

"Look, Garrison, I love you, and I know you love me," she said. "But I think my dad is right, and maybe we need to take a little time and figure it all out, you know?"

Garrison felt like a scorned puppy but tried not to show it. "I understand. Just know that regardless of what happens, I'll always be there for you."

They then embraced in a long hug. Meg squeezed him tight, then stepped away and started to leave the court.

"So, I'll see you at the game tonight?" Garrison asked.

She turned and gave a slight flirty grin, as if to say *Of course you will, silly*.

At that instant, Garrison felt a weight lifted from his shoulders. He didn't know if Wilder County would win the game that night, but he felt things would work out with Meg. That meant so much to him. Like his dad had told him a few nights ago, Garrison had a lot to be thankful for. He was now sure of that.

Chapter 17

Coach Van Gundy was an excellent coach for a number of reasons. One reason, in particular, was he practiced myriad offensive philosophies and sets, especially during the summer and early on during the season. This prepared his teams for the inevitable moment when the game plan would call for something drastic. When the Pirates got into postseason play, they could switch up their strategies to something his opponents would never see coming. It was akin to the Miami Dolphins unveiling the wildcat on an unsuspecting Patriots team in 2008. Coach Van Gundy could've waited for the regional tournament to pull out a surprise, but he knew how much a district tournament championship meant to his team. Tonight was the night.

Van Gundy met with his team in the locker room prior to the game. "Guys, we've tried several things against this Brooks County team. They're obviously big and tall so we've run out a big lineup at them twice. It didn't work either time. We've tried to outscore them in a high scoring affair, and that too has proven unsuccessful.

"Tonight, we're going to start a four-guard lineup: Garrison, Mike, Steph, and Faddyss." Everyone looked surprised, most of all Faddyss, who for the most part had only played mop-up minutes to that point of the season. "Kobe will still be out there at center. Danny and Andrew, you two will be the first guys off the bench. We're gonna run the old Dean Smith four-corners offense. I know we haven't been running it in practice at all recently, but I know you young men can execute it. When Brooks County gets impatient, and they will, we'll backdoor them to death. This will keep the score low, and they'll hopefully pucker down the stretch. We have to shorten the game to have a chance to win."

Coach went on to diagram the offense on the white board. As he did, the strategy behind it re-clicked with everyone from the summer practices and training camp. Garrison knew this was bold, but he also knew it was crazy enough that it just might work. The game plan was a quirk that could only be truly effective in high school. College and pro games have shot clocks, so four corners was not possible in those leagues. However, for Wilder County, it was a tremendous option to minimize the number of possessions, utilize their ball handling prowess, and take Lob Johnson completely out of the game.

As the players took the floor for the opening tip, it was easy for them to spot all the college scouts in attendance. Also strange was the huge Wilder County contingent. Usually they could only manage a handful of fans in the unfriendly confines of the Newmarket Boston Garden. Garrison Smith noticed none of it, as he was locked in on the mission at hand like a bird dog in a marsh.

Kobe Applegate leapt as high as he could for the opening tip, but Lob easily tapped the ball back to his point guard. Brooks County crossed the time stripe and uncharacteristically threw the ball out of bounds for a turnover. Faddyss inbounded the ball to Garrison, who dribbled up the court. Instead of attacking as he normally did, he dribbled away at the top of the key. Mike, Steph, and Faddyss flared out to the corners, and the next minute and thirty seconds turned into a game of keep-away.

Brooks County figured out what was going on and eventually got aggressive and greedy. As soon as that happened, Mike Williams cut backdoor and caught a perfect pass from Garrison. Williams laid it in to put Wilder County up 2-0.

The first quarter turned into a cat-and-mouse game that went by very quickly due to the lack of action. Brooks County tensely tried to run their normal offense, but they knew they had a limited amount of shots, so it disrupted their natural flow and confidence. With each Wilder County defensive rebound, Brooks County players and coaches showed visible frustration because they knew they had to wait as much as two minutes for their next opportunity. The rest of the first quarter they tried to match the four-guard lineup. But the back-door cuts kept burning them, and Wilder County led 10-4 when time ran out in the first.

To start the second quarter, Brooks County sagged back into a 2-3 zone defense, hoping to spur some action out of the Pirates. On their first possession, after holding the ball for twenty seconds, Garrison passed it to Steph on the wing. Steph, with no one on him, decided to launch a three. It bricked off the rim to Lob, who tossed an outlet pass to his point guard. On the subsequent possession Lob got it back in the post and shot a short hook over Kobe to cut the lead to 10-6.

Coach Van Gundy immediately called a timeout and pulled Steph out of the game. "Listen guys, I know it's tempting, but we need to run at least a minute off the clock before we attempt a shot unless we get a wide-open layup. That was too quick, Steph, and look what happened, they went right to work with Lob on the block. Danny, you're in. Flash to the high post every once and a while if they stay zone, to try and drag them in. If they do, the back door to Kobe or Mike from the wing will be there."

On the ensuing possession, Garrison brought the ball up the court, and surveyed the landscape. Brooks County refused to pick him up and packed it in deep again in the 2-3 zone. He passed to Faddyss, who kicked it right back to Garrison. He then held the ball for a full minute and twenty seconds about thirty-five feet from the basket without even dribbling the ball. Boos rained down on him from the Brooks County crowd. He just smiled, and even gave them a slight wave to encourage them on. He was in full control of the game, his team, and his own emotions.

Brooks County's coach finally blinked and told his guards to push the zone up to force the ball to move. At that moment, Danny Fisher cut to the free-throw line and received a bullet pass from Garrison. Lob moved up to guard the ball. Kobe cut to the basket but was covered by the collapsing wings of the zone.

Danny didn't panic, and instead reversed the ball to Mike in the far corner. He was all alone and launched a three pointer. This one found the bottom of the net, making the score 13-6 Pirates.

The rest of the first half went much the same way, and it was 15-10 at the break. Coach Van Gundy knew his team had a shot if they stayed with the plan. Brooks County remained in the zone, which for the most part prevented them from giving up any more back doors.

Garrison did get free for one layup, but that was the only bucket they scored in the third quarter. Lob got into a slight rhythm and scored all eight of his team's points in the stanza.

Now down 18-17 heading into the fourth, Coach Van Gundy grabbed his clipboard and drew up a play that would hopefully get Kobe Applegate a close look at the basket. They needed to maintain the lead if they wanted the four corners to remain effective. "Run the play! Let's go," he admonished his team as they broke the huddle.

Mike brought the ball across half-court and hesitated for a few seconds so Brooks County would immediately think four corners. The zone pressed up again. He passed the ball to Garrison on the right wing. Mike cut through but then moved his way back up to the high post where he set a back screen on an unsuspecting Lob Johnson. Kobe immediately broke for the basket.

At the same time Garrison feinted baseline then crossed over his defender and dribbled towards the middle of the floor. Lob fought through the screen and got within an eyelash of deflecting Garrison's lob pass to Kobe. Lob was a day late and dollar short as Kobe caught the pass, continued to elevate, and flushed it down with authority. Garrison had to suppress a smile for he knew he'd just checked one off the old bucket list: A lob pass over Lob Johnson. The Pirate faithful went crazy in the stands!

Wilder County stuck with the four corners offense in the fourth quarter. Brooks County exhibited fear at the thought of making a misstep, so the seconds and minutes melted away like sand through an hourglass. Steph redeemed himself as he got free on a backdoor to put the Pirates up 3 with under a minute left. Brooks County responded with a Lob Johnson thunderous dunk, plus a foul. He made the free throw to tie the game at 21 with only twenty-two seconds on the clock.

Coach Van Gundy drew up a clear out play for Garrison to take the ball into the teeth of the Patriots defense and make a decision: shoot or pass. Van Gundy could live with whatever his point guard decided to do.

As the players walked back onto the court Mike whispered to Garrison. "Take it right at Lob for the layup just like you did early in the season when you got that three-point play. You've got it!"

The Plank Brothers instinctively fist bumped. Garrison then gave a nod to Mike but didn't say anything. He was too dialed in. It was the first time he could remember not wanting to crap his pants from the pressure.

Steph Croom inbounded the ball. Garrison drove it down the court and crossed the time stripe with fifteen seconds left on the game clock. Initially Brooks County held back, but with ten seconds remaining another defender rushed Smith. He split the double team and dribbled to the top of the key at the eight-second mark, then made his move to the hoop. Andrew Wilson flanked him on the right side, and Mike flared out on the left wing. He saw the defense part like the Red Sea, and he drove the ball hard into the lane. As he elevated, he saw the towering Lob Johnson swat for the blocked shot. Garrison barely got the shot over his outstretched arm, and he watched as it caromed off the left side of the rim.

As Garrison fell to the hardwood, he saw Mike explode off the floor, grab the rebound, come down and make space with his rear end. He then sprang up and kissed the ball off the glass. It rattled around and hung on the rim for what seemed like forever. But as the horn sounded it fell through the net. Ballgame! The Wilder County Pirates were district tournament champions with a 23-21 victory!

Garrison made it to his feet and sprinted to his teammate and brother, Mike Williams.

"How'd you like that rebound, G-man?" An overjoyed Mike shouted.

"We're champions! We did it! Wooooooo!" Garrison yelled.

The two young men then embraced in a tight hug.

"I couldn't have done this without you, Garrison. Thank you for being there," Mike said.

"Anytime, brother. Anytime. You're the strongest guy I know! You're the strongest guy I know! What a rebound and stick back! That was awesome, bro!"

The two were soon mobbed by their teammates. Garrison embraced and slapped high fives with Coach Van Gundy. Wilder County fans stormed the court as well to join the celebration.

"Your plan worked, Coach! You're a genius," Garrison shouted over the hoots and hollers.

"A basketball coach is only as good as his players, Garrison. How many rings did Phil Jackson win without Michael Jordan or Kobe Bryant?" asked Van Gundy. He was a master of asking questions to make a point and to make his players think for themselves. Even in the midst of a postgame celebration, Coach Van Gundy held true to his tenets of teaching. Garrison laughed, thinking if his coach couldn't let go and enjoy this moment, then he never would. He and Van Gundy embraced once more.

Once Garrison broke free from his coach, he immediately hugged Kobe, Danny, Steph, and all his teammates. They eventually lined up to shake hands.

Lob was last in line and managed to not be a total ass. He merely said, "Good game, Garrison. See you down the road," then made his way off the court.

Garrison's eyes briefly found Wilder County assistant coach Johnny Woods adjacent to the Pirates' bench chatting with college recruiting coordinator Bob Robinson, who was known as a pipeline to NAIA schools like Freed-Hardeman and Bethel in West Tennessee. Smith could feel their eyes and conversation burning through him as the revelry continued. At that moment, a peace came over Garrison. He embraced his basketball future in his heart. Whether a scholarship player at a small school or a walk-on at a big school, he knew he was destined to play at the next level.

A boisterous Kobe interrupted his reflective moment. "G-Man, we did it! That LOB was sick! Can't wait to watch that over and over again!" he hollered.

Kobe kept talking, but Garrison looked for Meg. Garrison looked to his left, then to his right, finally he looked ten feet straight ahead, and there she was. Gorgeous, even dressed head-to-toe in pirate garb. Garrison ran towards her and lifted her off the ground with a resounding hug. Meg squeezed him right back.

There were more basketball games to play in the regional tournament and hopefully beyond. There were college decisions to make. There'd be spring days and nights dressed like a pirate at the Wilder County tennis courts to support Meg. There'd be graduation, the summer before college, pizzas to smash at Angelo's, and all sorts of challenges and opportunities. But right now, all of that was in the future. Garrison Elias Smith and the Wilder County Pirates were living in the moment, and it was perfect.

Acknowledgements

Plank Brothers came to fruition through love, help, and support from several contributors. First, thanks to my wife, Shay Taylor, for championing the project from day one. She helped tremendously with storyline ideas and character development, and she allowed me the time and space to get my creative juices flowing. She must have read the book twenty times during the editing journey. Shay never once complained when I locked myself in my office to "hammer out" a chapter while she cooked dinner with a cute baby girl crying on her hip and two young sons wrestling in the living room. This project would have been impossible to start, much less finish, without her.

I forwarded an early *Plank Brothers* draft to several friends and family members who read the book and let me know I had something brewing. That initial peer feedback motivated me to take the project all the way to market. Thanks to Michael Bailey, Andy Woods, Justin Woods, Justin Olivares, Derek Lusk, Shelton, and Mary Taylor for believing in Plank Brothers. I shared later drafts with Felton Jones, Marc Hubble, Hope Shelton, Lauren Woods, Amy Woods, and Kerry Kell; I appreciate their feedback as well.

Thank you to my longtime friend, Amy Murphy Curlis, for her *Plank Brothers* feedback and marketing ideation. Not all new novelists have the benefit of friendship and collaboration with someone as accomplished as Amy. During her executive-level career, she has advised CEOs, company presidents, physician leaders, boards of directors, and elected officials. She can now add hobby novelist to that list.

Thanks to my CCHS English teachers: Sandra Highers, Brenda Keller, and the late Martha Kelley. I fondly recall catching hand cramps writing Honors English papers during my four years of high school. I apologize for any comma errors in *Plank Brothers*. Thanks to Dr. Margrethe Ahlschwede, my English 111 and 112 professor at UT Martin. She encouraged creative writing and was impactful in my development.

When I first started writing *Plank Brothers*, there were so many unknowns. I did not have the story fully outlined when I started writing, and I was not sure what I would even do with the book once it was completed. Conversely, there was one thing written in stone from the beginning. I knew from day one that I would tap into Shelton's creative skillset for the cover art. Shelton possesses a keen creative eye. He is an artist in every sense of the word. I am thrilled with the vibe and look of the artwork and its connection to the heartbeat of the storyline.

When I completed the initial rough draft, I forwarded it to Ritch Bentley at Five Count Publishing. Ritch read the book and responded with half a page of positive feedback and two plus pages of critical feedback on things that needed to be corrected. At that moment, I knew I wanted to partner with Five Count to bring *Plank Brothers* alive. Ritch is methodical, dependable, and a true pro. His editing and writing skills took *Plank Brothers* to a level that I could not have gotten it to on my own. He jumped headfirst into the story and served as a partner and guiding light during the refining process. I am proud to be part of the Five Count Pub family.

Last, but certainly not least, I would like to thank my mom, Mary Taylor, who served as my librarian at Beech Bluff Elementary School. I fell in love with reading in her library during those formative years and was especially drawn to the sports book section. It is where I first read about and learned the histories of my favorite teams, the Miami Dolphins and New York Knicks.

Additionally, I had insider access to a secret room behind the main library that housed books from the old, defunct Beech Bluff High School. I devoured baseball lore and vividly remember reading books about Babe Ruth, Ted Williams, Jackie Robinson, Lou Gehrig, Roy Campanella, and many others. I loved everything about those old books, from the scent to the stamped check-out dates and signatures in the back. A love for books is truly a gift. That early love sparked the desire to eventually write my own sports novella.

Eric L. Taylor

About the Author

Eric L. Taylor is a husband, father, believer, salesperson, writer, martial artist, coffee sipper, sports junkie, history buff, wannabe R&B singer, and aspiring grill master. He lives in Middle Tennessee. For more, follow him on Twitter and Instagram at @ELTaylorMade.

More from Five Count Publishing

Looking for more great books to read? We have awesome books in the fiction, non-fiction, and children's categories. To find out more about each title and their authors, be sure to check out our website at www.fivecountpub.com, our Facebook page, or follow us on Twitter.

Fiction

Driftwood by Ray Bentley
No Rest for the Wicked by Vincent Alcaras
Cigar Boys: Stories from the Ashes by Lou Rossi
The Time Arrow by Sam Ruggiero

Non-Fiction

Anchor Up: Competitive Greatness the Grand Valley Way by Tim Selgo

Living Beyond Myself: An Out-of-Body Testimony by Roger P. Beukema Jr.

Make One Play: Impact Your Success by Tim Selgo

Children's Books

Darby the Dinosaur Series from Ray Bentley

Bubba Gator and the Gator Family Series from Ray Bentley

The Adventures of Daredevil Dylan Series from John LaFontsee

Octagon John Goes to Mars by Brad Faber

Made in the USA
Coppell, TX
21 September 2021